CODE DEEP BLUE

ROBERT J. STAVA

SEVERED PRESS
HOBART TASMANIA

CODE DEEP BLUE

1.

OCTOBER 27TH, 1943, 2015 HOURS.

"This way, Lieutenant Vanek. Mind your step."

The speaker was one of the Chief Petty officers, a bland-faced gentleman with lazy eyes and a southern drawl to match. Lieutenant Vanek pegged him from Georgia, or perhaps Alabama.

The Gleaves-class destroyer he'd just boarded, DD-505–better known as the *U.S.S. Exeter*–was getting underway as he was escorted up to the chart room in the aft section of the navigating bridge. Originally debarking from Philadelphia after extensive re-fitting, they'd left the naval base at Newport, Rhode Island, rather late due to the delay of a certain top-secret item that had been flown in from the Suffolk County Air Force Base.

The same item that was currently being carried up to the navigation room.

Lieutenant John Vanek, recently assigned to the Naval Intelligence unit stationed at Camp Hero, Montauk, was on a highly classified mission involving recent enemy activity–the official story was U-Boats–that had been detected off the coast of the United States.

The mission, detailed in the sealed envelope he carried under his arm, was code-named "Neptune's Reckoning". The top-secret technology it encompassed, which included instructions on use of the experimental equipment and wire-mesh hull surfacing the destroyer had been outfitted with over the previous five months, was aimed specifically at radically changing the course of the war in the North Atlantic.

Lieutenant Vanek was ushered into the cramped and Spartan cabin.

A chart table with flat files lined one wall, while next to it were three chronometers with a radar screen mounted overhead. A small desk took up the back wall, underneath an array of conduit pipes and an old-fashioned brass clock mounted there. There were only two officers waiting for him, the commander, Captain David Palmer, and his Executive Officer, Lieutenant Commander Richard Klein. The captain was seated at the small chart table while Lieutenant Klein leaned against the cabinet nearby, arms crossed.

The petty officer quietly closed the door behind Vanek.

Lieutenant Vanek removed his hat and saluted both men.

"At ease, Lieutenant," the captain said, "And, er, welcome aboard."

Lieutenant Vanek had been briefed on the two commanding officers he would be working with but this was the first time meeting them in person.

Captain Palmer was on the old side for a destroyer command, a reserve career officer from the Depression years who'd been reactivated for coastal duty. Although the tide of the war in the Atlantic was now steadily turning in their favor after the atrocious losses of the previous two years, seasoned captains were still hard to come by. In person he exuded an unflappable calm, with the weather-beaten, steady features of a sea-faring veteran who looked like he would hold his own in a storm.

Lt. Commander Klein, however, had the fine, thin-lipped look of a scholar, and even in repose his fingers tapped agitatedly against the desktop. Dark-haired, almost handsome in a square-faced, wide-eyed way, he immediately struck Vanek as the nervous type who would point the finger elsewhere a little too quickly when the chips fell. While his record was impeccable with all the dotted 'i's and crossed 't's in the right places, he had little battle experience to date.

Lt. Vanek kept his hat tucked under his arm until Captain Palmer gave him a nod and gestured to the chart table.

"All right, Lieutenant, don't keep us dancing on our toes," the captain said dryly. "Let's see what this business is about. We have less than two hours to reach our initial target co-ordinates."

Lt. Vanek broke the seal on the waterproofed envelope.

"This is going to sound a little like one of those pulp 'science fiction' tales, but here's what our orders are, Captain . . ."

A week earlier, when Lt. Vanek had been called into his commander's office, the subsequent briefing he'd received had sounded equally bizarre.

The mid-October morning was one of those sunny, bright ones, the kind when families should have been focusing on Halloween decorations and burning leaves in the backyard. But with the specter of war gripping the country and the reality of rationing, things were subdued this season. While kept out of much of the national newsreels, the stark reality of burning tankers and liberty ships off the eastern seaboard had local residents in dour spirits. Those were American boys and American ships the U-Boat's were torpedoing, and the Germans had made it clear they weren't going to be calling it quits anytime soon.

For the past six months, however, the war was finally beginning to turn in the Battle of the Atlantic with the appearance of destroyer escorts equipped with sonar. German U-boat losses were mounting. Increasingly, more ships were getting through with their critical supplies to England and the Mediterranean.

Still, it wasn't enough. The U-Boat 'wolf packs' were still extracting a terrible toll on convoys and the war department was pushing for more results. Faster.

Then along came the Hungarian, Anton Kovacs.

Kovacs, one of the pioneering scientists in electromagnetism, had been successfully smuggled out of the Nazi weapons program by partisans a year earlier in one of the more daring operations of the war so far. Kovacs had been working specifically on the application of electromagnetic coatings for both tanks and ships, the latter involving protection against torpedoes.

Which was where Lt. Vanek came in. With a degree in engineering from Case Western and with several patents under his belt at age 25, he'd enlisted and quickly been recruited by Naval Intelligence, initially to help with breaking the Enigma code: the cypher used by Nazi submarines for encoded communications. It'd quickly become apparent he not only excelled at creating innovative solutions for many of the more obtuse issues plaguing the Naval Department, he also had an aptitude for breaking rules and regulations, which made him a perfect candidate for the anti-submarine program, and more specifically, the highly unorthodox program involving Anton Kovacs.

If it succeeded, he was just the man who could make it work. If it failed, he was the perfect fall-guy.

Also, he spoke fluent Hungarian.

The program, carried out in the Philadelphia Naval Shipyard through the summer of 1943, involved outfitting the hull of the *U.S.S. Exeter* with a special metal mesh held in place by a unique adhesive paint developed by Kovacs. Hooked up to a tube-based electromagnetic field oscillator he'd also developed, the plan was to be able to set it to a frequency that would scramble the magnetic torpedoes currently in use by the Germans.

With additional modifications on the latest version of the device, Kovacs claimed it could do more than that: with the correct modulation it could render the ship invisible to radar.

It sounded utterly preposterous.

Still, he'd received his orders to proceed.

The shakedown cruise, originally scheduled for August, had been delayed by ongoing technical difficulties and setbacks. Lt. Vanek's only direct involvement had involved translating Kovacs' instructions into written documents, which grew increasingly bizarre the deeper he got into them. Then in early September, Kovacs abruptly disappeared from his Manhattan apartment and Lt. Vanek was instructed not to ask questions and simply get on with the translation work.

The program continued.

By the beginning of October, however, under increasingly skeptical queries from the Naval Department, it was clearly on the verge of being scrapped.

When Lt. Vanek had walked into his commander's office that October day, he was well aware of the rumors and was fully expecting the worst. Instead, he was faced with an even stranger surprise.

A top-secret mission known as: "Neptune's Reckoning".

Colonel Halstead gave him the key points in his usual gravel-voiced delivery, then let him read the brief.

Two months previously, a small transport, an obsolete destroyer and 3,000-ton tanker had vanished off the coast of Montauk, all within a single week. Then a sailing yacht, requisitioned for coastal patrol duty, had been found adrift near the lighthouse, with no sign of its crew.

At first the Navy suspected some sort of enemy saboteurs were at work. Coastal patrol aircraft had combed the area with no sign of any shipwrecks or debris.

Until they found a survivor from the destroyer who had been adrift for several days in a strong current that had taken him to Gardiner's Island. At first, he was dismissed as raving mad, as his account made little sense and told a horrifying—and grisly—tale.

Except that several details seemed remarkably similar to several historic accounts from the area, particularly the account of the whaling ship *Persia* and more disturbingly, that of a survivor of the wreck of the *HMS Tryton,* a frigate lost during the Revolutionary War.

"I'm not clear on how this relates to my current mission, sir," Lt. Vanek said after reading through the brief report and accompanying maps. "I'm just about to embark on the shakedown cruise with the new anti-submarine measures aboard the *U.S.S. Exeter*."

Colonel Halstead leaned forward and interlaced his fingers. His grey eyes were cold and unforgiving.

"The Navy's resources are limited, Lieutenant, and so is its patience with whack-a-doodle plans to combat the enemy, regardless of how well-intentioned they may be. The *U.S.S. Exeter* is an older vessel, and this business off Montauk is probably nothing special. Regardless, someone upstairs decided it was worth it to kill two birds with one stone."

Lt. Vanek had sat back, nodding to himself. The colonel was lying—he was positive of it—just as he was positive there was a lot more to "Neptune's Reckoning" than he was being told. Quite a lot more. Something very strange was going on out there off Long Island and the brass was uneasy about it. Someone had to go out there and prod the wasp's nest. And the subtext of the colonel's message was also clear: the *U.S.S. Exeter* was expendable.

Which meant he was too.

There was something else bothering him as well. Rumors about another secret program going on at Camp Hero.

One that he could only wonder might be tied into "Neptune's Reckoning".

All this he related to the two officers of the *U.S.S. Exeter*, omitting his own speculations and references to the Camp Hero rumors. To his credit, Captain Palmer simply nodded, and picking up his pipe from the desk, produced some tobacco and went through the sailor's time-worn ritual of patiently filling and lighting it. Lt. Commander Klein fished a cigarette from a pack in his breast pocket and lit it as well.

Lt. Vanek noticed the executive officer's fingers were shaking. It took him two tries to get the Zippo lighter to produce a flame.

Smoke quickly filled the small cabin, wreathing its way toward the ventilation grill in the ceiling. After a space, Captain Palmer spoke up.

"As you may well guess, Lieutenant," he said, puffs of smoke coming out the side of his mouth, "I'm not particularly enthusiastic about these new orders. Our original objective was to take our ship out for a shakedown cruise with this new anti-submarine get-up, which quite frankly, has turned out to be about as reliable as a one-eyed monkey in a hurricane. I wouldn't put much stock in it based on how things have gone these past few months. And yet in spite of such a shaky roll-out, now the boys upstairs have thrown this "Neptune's Reckoning" mission on top of it? I have two-hundred and sixty-seven crewmen I'm responsible for keeping alive here, Lieutenant, and while we're not on the A-list of the Navy's vanguard, I'd like to keep them that way."

Next to him the lieutenant commander was shaking his head as if contemplating a bad line-up at the racetrack.

"Yes, sir," Lt. Vanek replied. "May I speak frankly, Captain?"

"By all means," Captain Palmer replied, crossing his legs.

Lt. Vanek indicated the chart on the table next to him, "For the record, I didn't conceive or even advocate this mission. Quite the contrary. I was brought in strictly to facilitate the implementation and testing of Kovacs' "Anti-Magnetic Field Oscillation System" and nothing else. This business off Montauk Point is as much a left hook to me as it is to you."

"Some sort of new Nazi technology?" the Lt. commander offered.

Captain Palmer shook his head but didn't reply. Instead he took a couple pulls on his pipe and looked off into the distance. After a moment he grunted and looked up at Lt. Vanek.

"I doubt it. And I have a hunch you do too, Lieutenant. I've heard the rumors coming through the scuttlebutt. Nobody seems to want to touch whatever this new development is off Montauk." A whorl of smoke issued out of his pipe and rose up toward the vent. "At our current speed we should reach our patrol area in less than an hour. U-boats have been active in the area this week. Let's hope this time this that "AMFOS" system of yours works. At this point I don't have much more faith in it than the colonel. But tired as this ship is—and expendable as some may view her—she still has some teeth in her, new-fangled technology or not."

"I don't doubt it, sir," Lt. Vanek replied.

The captain stood up and turned to his second-in-command.

"Mr. Klein, take the lieutenant down to the mess for some coffee and make sure he's issued a lifejacket. I have a suspicion it's going to be an interesting evening."

2.

OCTOBER 27TH, 1943 2200 HOURS

As the *U.S.S. Exeter* cut southward through the Block Channel between Block Island and Montauk Point, the weather worsened into a blustery autumn squall. Lieutenant Vanek stood next to Captain Palmer on the main bridge, watching rain slash across the windows and thinking about how lucky he was to be an officer, privileged to be in one of the drier locations on the ship.

At least the wind was coming off the stern port quarter, meaning they were riding before the storm. Even so, the slim-hulled destroyer pitched and heaved sickeningly, the waves quickly reaching six to ten feet.

"Good odds we'll spot a U-Boat tonight," Captain Palmer was saying. The lights from the control station uplit his face in a spooky glow. "They like a little rough weather to slip past our patrols. Lately the bastards have come in as close as New York Harbor. All our aerial patrols are grounded right now so were down to our extra eyes. Hope that magic paint coating on the hull can take a licking—we're not through the worst of this weather just yet, though this squall should blow itself out before too long."

Lieutenant Vanek steadied himself as the ship lurched to starboard. On the deck below a wave broke, sending a curtain of seawater over the front turret. The watch on the fore deck were taking a beating. Even as he looked down, one of the crew lost his footing and would have been carried overboard if not for his safety harness.

"Heck of a night though, eh?" Captain Palmer said quietly, hands clasped behind his back. His face was steadfast and he had an air of unflappable calm about him, as if this was just another routine evening on another routine patrol.

Lieutenant Vanek felt his dinner roll over in his stomach, making a mental note of the proximity of the nearest head, which was in the captain's stateroom on the deck below. That he would do only as an absolute emergency as he had no desire to embarrass himself in front of the captain and especially Lieutenant Commander Klein, who stood on the opposite side of the bridge occasionally giving him a measured look as if waiting to see him fail.

No, Lt. Vanek knew there was more at stake than just a far-fetched anti-submarine technology here. His own future and career were on the line. He was also well aware that the same stubborn, adventurous, bold streak that often put him at odds with convention (and his superiors) made him expendable.

That was the damnable part of it . . . of himself . . . the compulsive drive to seek, to *understand* that which he didn't know. Even as a kid he'd always been the first to explore any rumored places in the neighborhood, to investigate abandoned houses, factories and caves. Often at personal risk to himself.

Now here he was, testing out a certifiably odd piece of cloaking equipment, one, which if it was successful, would make Allied ships all-but invisible to the German U-boat menace. Underwater at least, the German subs would be forced to resort to visual spotting, making them highly vulnerable.

Not to mention rendering their magnetic torpedoes useless.

"Anything coming up on radar?" Captain Palmer called out, his question directed at the operator at the center console back in the CIC center behind them.

"Nothing yet, sir," came the reply.

Lt. Vanek realized the captain was simply making talk to keep the men at ease.

The humid air in the bridge was an oppressive mix of sweat, ocean and the metallic reek of adrenaline. The shrill call of the bosun's whistle came through the ship's speakers, making Lt. Vanek wince.

"Now hear this: 8 o'clock sharp! The word before the mast: darken ship—the smoky lamp is out on all weather decks!"

"Is it necessary, sir?" the junior helmsman asked. "Hard to believe a U-Boat would be crazy enough to be on the surface in this weather!"

The lieutenant commander snorted, "We're in a *war*, Mr. Turpin. Never assume anything. Safety protocols aren't subject to your opinion, something you should consider before offering it in the future."

Captain Palmer raised a brow in response but didn't comment. Instead he motioned to Lt. Vanek. "Would you mind accompanying me to the chart room, I have a question or two regarding our search pattern." Turning to the lieutenant commander he said, "The bridge is yours, Mr. Klein."

Once back in the cramped room, Captain Palmer chuckled and went through his ritual of lighting his pipe. After he got it lit and tossed the match in the ashtray, he blew a whorl of smoke toward the ceiling and leaned back.

"He'll make a lousy captain, someday," Captain Palmer said out of the side of his mouth.

"I'm sorry, sir?" Lt. Vanek replied, though he knew exactly what he meant.

"Lt. Commander Klein. One of those prickly paper-pusher types who lives by his rulebook—at least when it's to his advantage. Has no clue whatsoever why the men can't stand him. Well, I didn't bring you back here to prattle on about my second-in-command. Since we have a little time, I just wanted a word with you regarding this AMFOS device."

"Sir?"

"I'll cut to the chase, Lieutenant. As I said before, I don't have much faith in your equipment—*any* untested equipment for that matter—and weather aside there's a good possibility we may run into the enemy sub that's been prowling these waters. But that's not what's really worrying me."

Lt. Vanek nodded, "Because you have an idea what's been *really* happening out here off the coast," he said, almost to himself.

Captain Palmer took a pull off his pipe and letting it out, contemplated an invisible spot on the opposite wall of the cabin, as if weighing carefully what he was about to say next. Smoke wreathed about the cabin and Lt. Vanek was overcome by the sensation of something fantastical: that whatever the captain was about to tell him, it was going to be in the realm of the otherworldly.

Or of nightmares.

"None of this leaves this room, are we clear?"

"Yes, sir."

"Would you care for a cup of coffee? The thermos next to you is kept fresh by the galley."

"Thank you, sir. Don't mind if I do."

Vanek took one of the porcelain cups and filled it. The captain waited until he was settled in again and continued.

"There's been talk," he began, "that something's out there, and I'm not talking U-Boats here, Lieutenant."

"What are we talking about? *Sea Monsters*?"

Lt Vanek meant it as a joke, but he realized the captain was serious.

"I don't know. Something is out there killing men, something that has nothing to do with Germans or this damned war. I'm not a superstitious man by nature, but I'd be a liar if I didn't admit this whole mission has me a little spooked, and I don't say that lightly. I ran into something similar about twenty years back."

Lt Vanek's ears perked up.

"You were here at Montauk?"

"Out of Narragansett, actually. Served with the Navy in the Great War. Was out of it nearly five years by then—1923. Hell of a summer. Montauk was just a ramshackle fishing village then on Fort Pond Bay. The Navy had already taken down the airship hangar on the bay, but the base was still there. I'd taken up with the Coast Guard as a pilot. We had a 38-foot picket boat—one of those open-cockpit interceptor ones—used mainly to deal with 'rum runners'. It was the Prohibition, mind you, and Montauk was a hotspot for the booze smugglers. They were running circles around us, of course. Not much one boat can do against a flotilla. But that summer, that summer everything changed."

"What changed?" Lt. Vanek prompted, when the captain's gaze went distant into the landscape of memory for a minute. According to the briefing file, Captain Palmer was 52, putting him at twenty years younger at the time he was talking about.

"Eh? Oh yes! Well, starting around June or so, we started to see a drop in the volume of smuggling. It was more or less word of mouth—smugglers weren't about to report their troubles to the police or Coast Guard. But people talk. Boats were mysteriously disappearing off Block Island

and Montauk. At first, they thought it was a competitor moving in on the action. By July 4th weekend it had ground to a standstill.

"Then the stories leaked in. Fantastic ones, hard to credit. Some told of a giant sea monster—a Kraken—lurking off the coast. One sailor swore he saw a dragon the size of a blue whale breach and swallow a fishing boat in one gulp, another where a waterspout grew arms and a face, the air turning a sickly greenish black all around it as it destroyed a small tramp freighter. Yet another bizarre version told of nightmarish mermaids attacking a schooner, eating the crew alive.

"It was hard to credit these things and there were more than a few murmurings that maybe the Canadians were slipping some kind of hallucinogen in the liquor. I myself saw one of the smuggler's boats that was found capsized off the Point. At first, we thought it was a sunken boat that had been tossed up out of the depths – God knows how many wrecks there really are in the area, but when we traced the name, we discovered it had dropped off a cargo just a few days earlier. Damn thing looked like it had been at the bottom of the ocean for decades. That wasn't even the strangest part."

Lt. Vanek sat back.

Is he going to pull my leg with a really tall one? he wondered.

It was stranger than he could have guessed.

3.

OCTOBER 27TH 1943, 2205 HOURS.

"You won't find any reference of the story I'm about to tell you in any official record. None at all." Seeing Lt. Vanek's eyebrows go up, he added, "Yes, it's quite a story."

Lt. Vanek couldn't resist a little poke. "And this is where you tell me 'every word of it is true'?"

Captain Palmer snorted, but an amused smile tugged at the corner of his mouth. "As a matter of fact, *yes*. It was told to me by my father, who witnessed it. This incident goes back to the winter of 1903, March 2nd to be exact, when it happened. It had been an odd winter that year, with unseasonal warm spikes that saw temperatures in the 50s and 60s during February.

"That particular day had been in the low 60s right after a cold spell and much of Eastern Long Island spent it locked down in dense fog. Around nine p.m. along comes a freighter of 5,071 gross tons out of Bremen known as the *Wilhelm Koenig*. She was carrying mostly textiles and machinery, a few dozen passengers and assorted wares from Iraq and Iran. There was nothing to suggest anything unusual happened on the voyage across. The last known contact was from a passenger ship eastbound out of Boston near the outer banks, which exchanged weather information two days prior.

"Something *did* happen, however, between there and its ill-fated rendezvous with the *U.S.S. Bronson*, an early DD type destroyer on its way to Rhode Island. *What*, exactly, seems to be in the realm of the *unworldly*.

"My father, Warren G. Palmer, was a chief gunner on the *Bronson*, under Captain Edgar Lawrence. They were on a supply run to Narragansett from New York. According to him, at just past nine that evening, the *Wilhelm Koenig* was spotted emerging from the fog on an erratic course north of the Ambrose to Nantucket traffic lane. At first the two ships were on opposite courses that would pass less than a hundred yards apart—a little tight for the destroyer captain's comfort. What put them on full alert, however, was what state the other ship was in."

"What state was that?" Lt Vanek asked.

"Like it had been underwater," Captain Palmer replied, "for a *long* time. Whole sections of the hull rusted, coated with seaweed and barnacles."

"That sounds . . ."

"—farfetched. I know. But that wasn't the worst of it. The worst of it was the crew. Or what was left of them. They were rotted, like they too had been underwater for a long spell. For all their ghastly appearances, they should have been dead. But they weren't."

Lt Vanek grinned and winked, as if he'd heard a variation or two of this tale before. Usually in a seaside bar when too many drinks had made the rounds.

"So, if you can imagine it . . . an uncomfortably warm winter evening in 1903: you're on one of those early, clunky, coal-powered destroyers. The tepid air reeks of brine and coal. The ocean is unnaturally still—scarcely a ripple on its surface. You're already spooked by the weird weather and fog, and then, out of the writhing darkness emerges this apparition, this seaman's nightmare. The alarms sound—all hands to battle stations!

"The captain could hardly credit what he was looking at through his binoculars. He saw the crew—corpses every one of them—all watching the *U.S.S. Bronson's* approach, as if *expecting* them. Even the passengers were on deck: although none of this will ever appear in any official reports; years later in a local newspaper interview with Captain Lawrence's widow she'll allow the reporter to look through Captain Lawrence's private journal, with all its grisly implications.

"Every one of them, he noted, had two things in common. One is their eyes—the silvery homicidal glow of an Angler fish. The other is the insidious voices, barely above a whisper yet carrying across the water. The still, dead water. The accounts all agree on one thing; the voices kept telling secrets, terrible secrets personal to each man.

"For Captain Lawrence, it's about his dead brother Edward, who died skating on a nearby river when they were kids, after they'd promised their parents they wouldn't. Edward went through the ice—it was late in the winter—and he was swept away under the current. The captain never told a soul. Not even his wife. About how he'd panicked and hid in the woods, mewling like a little baby, the last shriek of his brother as he went under still ringing in his ears.

"Impossibly, he was hearing his dead brother's voice again: *Edgar . . . why . . .?* Followed by: *I'm coming for you Nate . . . I'm going to wrap my cold dead hands around your . . .*

"Captain Lawrence didn't get any more specific other than to note he swore the entire crew to silence or risk being court-martialed, but the handwriting was shaking to the point of being illegible. Despite the gag order, some of the crew *did* talk—they always do."

Lt. Vanek crossed his legs, oblivious to the roll of the ship. For all his taciturn demeanor and officer's authority, Captain Palmer was a sailor of the old stripe: the kind that relished a good seafaring tale. No doubt he had given enough talks to know a story junkie when he saw one.

"What did they say?" Lt. Vanek asked.

"Well, the three accounts I heard, including my father's, said the same thing: the *Wilhelm Koenig* veered toward them and sped up. Captain Lawrence gave the order to go 'Flank speed" and swerved into them to avoid a collision, but it was too late. The cargo ship rammed the destroyer a glancing blow amidships—which might have been catastrophic for both — but the German vessel's decayed hull all but imploded. The *U.S.S. Bronson* hauled off to starboard and within minutes the *Wilhelm Koenig* sank with its terrible crew, vanishing within the misty waters."

Lieutenant Vanek laughed outright. "Quite a story," he said, raising his mug. "And no doubt a curse and a buried treasure to go with it, no?"

"Well, *no*, actually," Captain Palmer said, looking around uncomfortably. He'd done it again. Every time he got into relating a story, he had a habit of running off at the mouth, embellishing and adding extraneous details. His father used to belittle him about it, calling it "Accessorizing". "Davy's been accessorizing his stories again!" his father would tell his mother, often referring to him in the third person while he was standing right there. Even as a kid, Palmer sensed it was a demeaning term, one implying he was *a sissy*, a word his grade school buddy Jackson used judiciously.

"Sounds like quite a tale," Lt. Vanek said, sipping his coffee. "Except one or two things."

"One *major* thing is wrong with the story," Captain Palmer agreed. "Which makes it a bunch of horseshit."

Lt. Vanek shook his head, "Aside from the ship's condition? The dead passengers?"

"The *ships*," Captain Palmer offered.

"I don't follow."

Captain Palmer tapped his pipe. "The *weight* of the ships. Even if you accept the dead crew and impossibly decayed freighter, it couldn't have happened like it did. The *U.S.S. Bronson* was a destroyer of roughly 600 tons, fully loaded. As I said, the *Wilhelm Koenig* was over 5,000. Even in a 'decayed' condition, there's no way it could have rammed that destroyer without inflicting serious damage. And there was no report of any damage when the ship arrived in Newport the next day. No, I knew that tall tale or not, that version of events (including my own father's) didn't add up. Then I came across a manifest in the National Archives a couple months back. The *Bronson* was shy four torpedoes when she came into port."

"They had torpedoes back then?" Lieutenant Vanek asked.

"The first guided torpedoes were patented in 1877. Not very reliable, but they could sink a ship if they worked, though you had to get in dangerously close range," the captain replied. "The official report stated they were used in training, but I have another theory: they were used to sink that ship."

Lieutenant Vanek looked disappointed. "You're killing a perfectly good ghost story, sir."

Captain Palmer blinked. "I am? Well, there it is," he said, "but it only makes sense. If the freighter was in the condition the story claimed, it was probably a slow-moving target. Even the early destroyers were maneuverable. My guess is before the freighter came too close, Captain Lawrence hauled off and gave the order to sink the *Wilhelm Koenig*, then fabricated a cover-up."

"What makes you think that?" Lieutenant Vanek asked, still not buying any of this from the look on his face. "Aside from the missing four torpedoes?"

"Because of these."

Reaching into his breast pocket, he pulled out four square photos and laid them on the desk.

"Taken from my father's Brownie camera. I found these in his safe deposit box after he passed away."

The photos were of poor quality—they'd been taken at night with a handheld—but the first two were enough to make out a freighter in terrible condition, its running lights reflecting off the still water. There were dozens of tiny lights on the deck, though whether the 'silver eyes' Captain Palmer relayed, or some other phenomena, it was impossible to tell. Either way, the effect was spooky. The third shot showed the bright flash of an explosion on the ship's starboard side, the fourth one half of the capsized hull, with odd, tentacle-like objects in the water. They were blurred, as if in motion.

Something about them raised the hair on the back of Lt. Vanek's neck.

He flipped them over.

On the back, in neat cursive letters, was written:

March 3rd, 1903:
Wilhelm Koening
God forgive us.

Lt. Vanek placed the photos back on the desk. In his mind the skeptical side of him was seeing a bunch of holes in this story, starting whether the ship in the photos was in fact the *Wilhelm Koenig*. It might be. It might not be. But he didn't see any point in challenging Captain Palmer's assumptions.

He tapped the coffee mug with his fingers. "An interesting tale, Captain. But I'm not entirely sure how this relates to what happened in twenty-three?"

"Nor am I. But one is suggestive of the other, I think."

Lt. Vanek considered that. "I don't understand. Did they ever catch that thing? Was there any hard evidence?"

Captain Palmer puffed on his pipe, weighing his answer. "That's the odd thing. There was a mad rash of deaths and missing sailors . . . then, just like that, it stopped."

"*Stopped*?"

"Stopped."

"I don't understand. Was there a formal investigation? An inquiry?"

Captain Palmer leaned back and tapped his pipe, which had gone out. Then he leaned forward, arms on knees. "Now that's the odd thing about it too. It's like a kind of collective amnesia set in. The whole matter dissipated out of the news, talk died out, life went on."

Lt. Vanek was perplexed. "How is that possible? Even the press?"

"Even the press. Like one of those hypnotist tricks where you forget everything when you wake up."

"But *you* didn't forget."

"No, not all of it. But a lot of it is pretty hazy in my mind, like a bad dream you had weeks back. I've thought about that over the years. Maybe because I wasn't from around here and was only stationed at the Fort Pond base briefly before returning to Rhode Island."

He tapped out his pipe and stood up, signaling the talk was over. From the smoother motion of the deck under his feet, Lt. Vanek sensed the squall had eased up as well, as if in deference to Captain Palmer's calm demeanor.

"Didn't mean to bend your ear so far," the captain said, "but I thought you should know about that, being that we may be about to tweak the proverbial sleeping tiger by the tail tonight. Call it an old sailor's hunch."

"Hopefully that's all it is, sir. We'll test out this new AMFOS successfully, get back to port and call it a night."

The ghost of a smile appeared on the captain's face. "Well, let's hope you're correct—"

He was interrupted by a tap on the bulkhead door.

"Enter."

The Chief Petty Officer who'd escorted Lt. Vanek aboard earlier poked his head in.

"Mr. Klein's respects, sir. We've picked up a spook 800 yards off the port bow, heading one-four-one!"

"Very good, Mr. Stevens. Tell Mr. Klein I'll be there directly. Tell him to plot a course to follow, but not engage."

"Aye-aye, sir!"

He turned to Lieutenant Vanek. "Well, well, Lieutenant. Looks like we're going to find out whether this new rig of yours works even sooner than I expected."

Lt. Vanek nodded, feeling the first real twinge of nerves since embarking on this mission. Up to this moment it was all an anticipated event in the future. Now it was really happening.

They'd gone through the basic procedures earlier, but Lieutenant Vanek was hardly 100% confident. The first run-through had shorted out the electric system and forced them to reset the breakers while the ship wallowed in the swells. The unit drew an alarming amount of power, requiring the *Exeter* to have her generators completely overhauled. The second time they'd cycled up the electromagnetic field oscillator the lights had dimmed precipitously but without overloading the system, the makeshift and oddly futuristic circular monitor showing a pulsing halo around a generic outline of a ship's hull.

Back on the bridge, the tension was palpable. Gone was the relaxed demeanor of the crew. Now they reminded Lt. Vanek of bull terriers, alert for prey. Even Lieutenant Commander Klein had his nose up, as if sniffing out the U-Boat in the dark.

With the ship's running lights off, the ocean was an intimidating panorama of blackness, broken only by the wave crests in the diffused moonlight bleeding through the cloud cover.

For a fleeting second, Lt. Vanek wondered about the collective fear of all these men crammed together in this metal ship, all that deep-rooted terror seething behind two-hundred and sixty-seven facades . . . it was a bizarre thought: *what might that possibly look like?*

"Mr. Klein?" Captain Palmer queried, a list of questions implied.

"Sonar sweeping beam to beam, sir! He's holding steady, no indication he's spotted us." The sonar's hollow *ping* was followed shortly by a deeper *pong* as the signal bounced off the sub's hull.

"Mr. Bremen?" the captain asked. He was addressing the junior officer hunched over the oscilloscope monitor like some kind of military gypsy peering at a crystal ball.

"So far so good, sir. Haven't blown the breakers to Tripoli yet, at least."

"Glad to hear that." He turned to Lieutenant Vanek, "I think we'll ease up on him nice and slow. You think we're really invisible to him, Lieutenant?"

"That's how it's supposed to work, sir. Though he can hear our engines. And the sonar pings, of course. But he shouldn't be able to pick up on our hull signature, nor get a lock on us with torpedoes."

"*Supposed* to work," Lt. Commander Klein said under his breath.

Captain Palmer ignored him and picked up the interior communications mic. His voice was as droll and confident of someone out for a Sunday stroll. "This is your captain. You may be wondering about our status. We're tracking an unidentified vessel, possibly an enemy U-Boat. All hands man your battle stations." Dropping it back in its cradle, he said, "Ahead two thirds, Mr. Larkin," he said, addressing the helmsman. "Let's close the distance and see what happens."

The destroyer picked up speed, sluicing through the low rolling swells the squall had left behind. Through the overhead loudspeakers came the various ship's stations calling back in, their voices canned and tinny:

"Front gun, manned and ready, sir!"

"Boiler room, manned and ready, sir!"

"Aft deck . . ."

Lieutenant Vanek tuned them out, focusing instead on the screen of the oscilloscope, its pulsing glow hypnotic in the dim light of the bridge.

"He's leading us toward deeper water, sir," came the voice of the navigator, "right towards the Hyborian Canyon, sir!"

Captain Palmer frowned, wondering about the U-Boat's intent. Probably heading toward the main shipping lane between New York and Boston, though there were no convoys in the area tonight. The U-Boat captain wouldn't know that, of course.

For a space of five or six minutes it was all tense silence, except for the monotonous *ping* of the sonar.

Then it stopped.

A clang and a curse came from the CIC room behind them, as if someone tripped up a chair.

"Lost contact, sir!"

"*What*!?" Captain Palmer snapped.

"I-I don't know, sir. One moment it was there—the next it was gone!" The sonar operator sounded flustered.

Lt. Commander Klein dashed over to the door of the CIC room. "Double check!"

"I *am*, sir!"

There came a loud smack of hand on metal.

"Nothing!"

"Impossible!" the lieutenant commander said, as if to himself. "He was well within range . . . check again, dammit!"

"I-I."

"Reset the system!" Lt. Commander Klein's voice took on a shrill quality.

"I'm trying!"

"Don't just *try*, just—"

"Got it!" an answering *ping . . . pong* from the sonar confirmed this.

"Everything back in order, Mister Klein?" the captain asked, his voice even.

"Aye, sir!"

"Bridge, we have another spook on radar!" chimed in the radar operator. "Off the starboard bow, nine-hundred yards!"

"Radar contact! Radar contact!" echoed the watch officer.

"Well, what have we got?" the captain asked, after a moment.

Lt Commander Klein had already moved toward the bridge windows, scanning with his binoculars.

"Don't know," the radar operator called back. "Could be a fishing vessel. Or a conning tower."

"That's a U-Boat, sir," Lt. Commander Klein, said. "Just caught the splash of the conning tower. She's diving."

"Mr. Bremen?" Captain Palmer asked, addressing the radar operator.

"Appears to be heading one-four-zero! Speed, nine knots!"

Captain Palmer turned to the ensign at his side. "Notify dispatch. Have engaged two U-Boats. Twenty miles south-southeast of Montauk Point. Heading one-four-zero."

"Aye sir!"

He looked over at Lt Commander Klein, who was pressed up against the bridge windows.

"Mr. Klein?"

"He's under. Looks like—"

"—they've both changed course ten degrees, heading one-five-one, sir!" the sonar operator interrupted. The sonar *pings* and *pongs* sang a counterpoint chorus.

"Adjust our course likewise," the captain instructed.

"Aye-aye, sir!"

A momentary silence settled over the crew as they stayed in pursuit. For Lieutenant Vanek it felt like a quiet interlude—except for the sonar—though the tension in the air was still thick. After a few minutes, sonar picked up another ping, this time twelve-hundred yards off to port.

"Wolfpack, sir?" Lt. Commander Klein offered.

"It would appear so, Mr. Klein," Captain Palmer replied. Now he was faced with a new dilemma: they were one destroyer against three subs. The nearest Naval assistance was a cruiser at Providence, unless they called in support from the air base at Montauk, or the Coast Guard cutter at Fort Pond Bay.

"I've just picked up two more spooks, sir, just past the first contact. Correction, *three* more." The sonar chorus took on an agitated confusion of sounds.

Captain Palmer felt the first icy trickles of concern seep into his thoughts.

An uneasy silence fell over the bridge.

"They've stopped, sir," the radar operator said, his voice unusually loud in the silence.

"*Stopped? All* of them?"

"Aye, sir! All six."

"Stop engines!" the captain barked.

The sonar pings took on an oddly synchronized rhythm.

Like the pulse of a heartbeat, Lieutenant Vanek noted, *how odd is that?*

Captain Palmer's stories crept back into his thoughts. What exactly in the hell was out there?

"Message to dispatch," Captain Palmer said. "Request air support. Mr. Bremen, target depth?"

"All six are at fifty feet, sir!"

Shallow enough for torpedoes, Lt. Vanek thought. *But of course, the entire crew would know that. They were facing six enemy subs. The stern tubes could fire two at once. Twelve all together.*

Like facing a firing squad.

The silence drew out.

Then: "Mister Klein, tell the crew to prepare depth charges. Set pattern for fifty feet but be ready to change that on a moment's notice. Helm, flank speed and set a course for the right-most sub."

"*Sir?*"

"You heard me correct, Mister Klein. Let's see what this old tub has in her. And let's pray to God this anti-sub device of yours really works, Mister Vanek!"

The destroyer surged forward at an oblique angle toward the enemy submarines, with Lt

Commander Klein and the watch officer scanning fervidly for any telltale signs of torpedoes.

"Range?" Captain Palmer asked.

"Seven hundred yards and closing, sir."

"Any movement?"

"No sir."

Lieutenant Vanek's hands tightened behind his back. *That's odd. They're acting like sitting ducks. If the subs weren't moving, it was all but impossible to dive unless they blow their ballast tanks.*

"Mister Klein?"

"Nothing yet. Crew on deck awaiting order to launch depth charges, sir."

"Shortly, Mister Klein. Lieutenant Vanek?"

"Fine so far, sir." The monitor continued to give off its pulsing amber glow. Meanwhile the sonar took on an erratic, almost frantic singsong as their angle of approach changed to the U-Boats.

"Range?" the captain called out again.

"Four hundred yards and closing, sir!"

"Change in any of the enemy positions?"

"No sir!"

The tense air in the bridge tightened even further. The features of every crewman looked etched in stone—the primordial faces of hunters closing in on a dangerous prey. Even Captain Palmer's fatherly features took on a menacing cast.

"Depth charges ready, Mister Klein?"

"Aye-aye, sir!"

"Standby to fire, on my command!"

"Two-hundred yards and closing, sir!"

"Damn, what are they waiting for?" the junior officer next to Lt. Vanek—Bremen—muttered under his breath.

"Sitting ducks," said someone nearby.

"One-hundred yards . . . seventy-five . . . fifty . . ."

"*Ready*, Mr. Klein!"

Something was bothering Lieutenant Vanek, however. Something about the pattern of the subs reminded him of . . .

"They've . . . they've disappeared again, Captain!"

The destroyer gave a sudden sideways lurch followed by the groan of tortured metal, as if it had run aground on an iron sandbar. A second jolt followed, sending the men on the bridge stumbling. From the decks below someone was screaming.

"Oh, God, *what is that!?*" said Officer Bremen.

As the bridge tilted even further, eyes went wide with terror as they saw what was coming up out of the ocean.

4.

OCTOBER 27TH, 1943 2245 HOURS

Lt. Vanek felt his entire upper body break out in goosebumps as his eyes took in the horror unfolding before him. It was all but impossible to process, and almost humorous in the frantic ways his brain attempted to rationalize what was happening: the ocean around the bow of the destroyer was broken by a set of gargantuan blue-black jaws that were a terrifying hybrid of mechanical and organic.

Double the width of the destroyer, the teeth dwarfed those of the megalith shark he'd once seen on display at the Museum of Natural History. The skin around the mouth had a glistening, metallic quality to it.

Like the hull plates of a German submarine.

For a ludicrous moment, Lt. Vanek was convinced this must be some kind of bizarre Nazi super-weapon. He could see the luminous white-pink interior of the mouth, which was also lined with irregular teeth, suggesting a titanic shark or lamprey eel. Like a cavernous trap door opening, ocean water cascaded into it, led by the bow of the destroyer. And toward the top, an array of cobalt blue orbs that must be the thing's misshapen eyes.

The myths and legends were true! There are sea monsters! Lt. Vanek thought as the deck tilted even more precipitously, causing anything still loose on the bridge to go tumbling forward, including the crew members. *I'm just witnessing the God-almighty terrible truth and am about to die for it!*

Along with the groan and shriek of metal plates and parts coming loose—the awful death cries of a ship being destroyed—came the screams of the men. Next to him, Captain Palmer said nothing, his bared teeth and terror-widened eyes saying it all for him, while Klein lost his grip and went falling forward, head ricocheting off the radar console with a sickening crunch before he fell through the fractured bridge windows and tumbled forward down the deck, arms akimbo like a rag doll.

Three other bridge officers quickly joined him.

This isn't possible! This isn't happening! Vanek tried to tell himself.

There are no such things!!!!

He squeezed his eyes shut, trying to force it all out of his head. To make it not be so.

For a second he thought he felt something: a hiccup, or a *blink* in his mind as if . . . then he felt a shuddering lurch and opened his eyes again as the deck tilted forward, the horrific maw swallowing them. Men were screaming all over, metal clanging and snapping—a loose guy wire from the mast head whipped by the bridge and shattered windows, the radar array tumbling over in a shower of exploding electric arcs, trailing cables.

Down they went, with a slowness resembling a stop-action nightmare. The flickering ship's lights, foaming water and moonlight only enhanced the effect.

When the bow of the ship was in the thing's mouth, the jaws clamped shut, cutting through steel plating, human bodies. Next to him, with the tilting of the deck now extreme, Captain Palmer was now standing on the steering column, gripping the skipper's chair to keep from falling down through the bridge windows. Lt. Vanek had instinctively done the same, sliding over to the port bridge entrance where the steel door swung lazily, hanging on to the frame for dear life.

If none of this was taxing their sanity enough, a series of eel-like tentacles thick as telephone cables and ending in a spray of writhing worm-like appendages shot out of the water on either side of the ship, plucking random crew members off the tilting ship like they were choice morsels.

Lt. Vanek saw one sailor get yanked past the bridge and crushed to a pulp, his innards erupting out of his mouth as his midsection was squeezed.

Based on the amount of disruption in the water, whatever was behind the jaws must have been a leviathan. The entire ship was shifted one way then another, accompanied by more tearing of steel plating and screeching. The front gun turret let loose and tumbled off to starboard, trailing cables and piping like the guts of an eviscerated fish. Several of the tentacles burst into the bridge, one seizing the last enlisted man with them and tossing him away. Captain Palmer drew his sidearm with one hand, firing several times point blank at the nearest tentacle—it snapped about in response and whacked him aside and into the captain's chair.

Mercifully, Lt. Vanek saw his eyes roll up as he lost consciousness, falling down through the windows to join the destruction below.

Lt. Vanek guessed he only had seconds left to live. One of the tentacles splayed its appendages at him in a way that suggested a hissing snake. In that moment he saw bulbous orbs in and around them that he took for eyes, though they looked more like glowing tumors that had erupted out of the blue-black skin.

One of the tentacles snagged his thigh, with it a sensation like several sharp needles puncturing his skin. Screaming, Lt. Vanek grabbed at it and managed to rip it aside, kicking it away as it snatched at him a second time.

Another tentacle shot through above him in the doorway and seizing his opportunity, he hauled himself past it. There was a sickening moment as he saw himself tilting some sixty feet above the ocean surface.

The decision to jump was taken away from him as the ship was wrenched in the opposite direction, catapulting him out into the darkness.

He remembered flailing his arms, a gut wrenching feeling as if plunging into an abyss, then the impact of slamming into the water, obliterating all other thought.

***

He snapped back to consciousness at once. At least it seemed that way.

Lieutenant Vanek was floating in the open water, teeth chattering from hypothermia, in a regulation Navy-issue life jacket he had no recollection of putting on. His body was numb in a post impact kind-of-way: the chill of the ocean water was a soothing balm. Like drifting in the womb.

To the east, the sun was on the cusp of breaking over the horizon, meaning he'd been knocked out for seven hours or more. His thoughts felt packed in dense wool, as if the cold had seeped into his brain cells, calming them to sleep. He had trouble focusing on *why* he was here, or exactly what had occurred.

None of it was good. That much he knew.

He felt something off . . . had his brain been injured in the fall?

A darkness. A slurry, ill feeling at the back of his thoughts. Like an oil slick.

He tried to focus on his current situation.

In another circumstance it might have been something: the fiery birth of a new day as the sunlight shot through the underbelly of the clouds clutching the horizon, the slow-rolling surge of the ocean waves drawing him along.

To his death, most likely.

He was alone in the vast sea, no sign of the *U.S.S. Exeter* or the two-hundred and sixty-seven crew that were alive, breathing and going about their duties just hours before. Men of all walks of life, ages and ranks.

Gone. Vanished from the earth. An entire, efficiently functioning enclosed world and its vessel, erased.

Now it was just him and his life jacket.

Drifting.

Where am I? he thought. *Did I drift further out into the Atlantic Ocean? Or the Block Island Channel?* From his low angle it was impossible to tell. He could be halfway to North Carolina, for all he knew.

Surely someone must be looking for them . . .?
No? A U.S. Naval destroyer on a secret mission?

Vanished. Subtracted.

Just me. Floating away to oblivion.

A certain lassitude had come over him, which he didn't mind for a change. Lt. Vanek had always been as persistent as a bull terrier when it came to tackling any obstacle in life. Whether it was his first motorcycle, his high school sweetheart or his current special section assignment, John Vanek went at his target with an unwavering surety of purpose that was unnerving to many. He never gave up until he'd achieved his objective.

Until now.

Fate wasn't about to let him off the hook that easily, however. Even as Lt. Vanek felt himself begin to drop back into the deeper well of unconsciousness, an approaching buzz nudged him out of it. At first, it was indistinct, with the water lapping at his head and occasionally swamping his ears, but it continued to grow, persistent, until the unmistakable drone of the twin Pratt & Whitney aircraft engines turned to a dull rumble.

As the sunrise burst into a full-fledged morning his eyes rolled up to see the PBY Catalina flying boat zoom overhead, the golden rays glinting off its Perspex windows as it banked past. It didn't seem possible they could have spotted him in the vastness of the ocean, but this particular Search & Rescue crew was on rotation back from the war in the Pacific and were experts at finding survivors lost in the vastness of the sea.

Time took on a slurry quality.

Lt. Vanek wasn't sure if he remained afloat for a few more minutes or hours, only that his next lucid recollection was strapped into a cot on the Catalina, the warm sun magnified by the Perspex fuselage blister while someone—a medic apparently—tended to his injuries.

"Holy moly, what *happened* to him?" one of the crew asked, looking over the medic's shoulder. His voice was nearly lost in the hum and rattle of the aircraft's interior.

"I'm not sure . . ." the medic replied in a terse voice. Lt. Vanek heard a snick and felt a tug as his pant leg was cut away. "It looks like some kind of punctures." The medic's eyes noted the lieutenant bars on Lt. Vanek's collar. "Sir, can you tell me what happened to you?"

Lt. Vanek's head was splitting and his throat felt like it had been rubbed raw with sandpaper. "We . . . were attacked."

"By a U-Boat?" the medic asked. It was highly unlikely it could be anything else.

"That's what we thought. At first," Lt. Vanek's words came out in a hoarse whisper. "It was a . . . a *monster*. Ate the entire damn ship."

He knew even as he said it, it sounded ridiculous. The *whatya make of that* look the medic gave the crewman behind him said it all.

"Of course, of course," the medic said. "You've obviously been through quite a shock. This should calm you down a bit."

Lt. Vanek saw the syringe and struggled against his restraints. "No! I need to contact my department. We were on a . . . a—" he cut himself off, realizing that saying anything more would violate his orders.

Within a minute, the world took on a dreamy cast.

Before it did, however, he felt an odd sensation—as if something *writhed* in his brain.

A black spot appeared at the edge of his vision, and for one horrific moment the faces of the men in front of him shriveled and caved-in, eyeballs bursting and maggots erupting from their mouths, noses and ears.

Lt. Vanek tried to scream but couldn't. The world blurred and faded.

The crewman, leaning forward with one hand on the interior bulkhead blinked. For a split second their passenger's eyes had taken on a strange look, like an alien fish.

Glowing blue.

5.

OCTOBER 31ST, 1943 0900 HOURS

Lt. Vanek snapped awake.

His first reaction was to sit up but found he couldn't. He was bound tightly to the bed. The small infirmary ward he was in was empty, he could see that much. There were only a dozen beds in the room—standard cast-iron ones—bathed in the golden rays of sunset. It was quiet except for the faint, tinny sound of a radio coming from a room by the entrance and the intermittent rattle of windowpanes from the ocean breeze.

He tried to take stock of what happened, but everything seemed fuzzy, as if his memories were buried in deep piles of grey sheep's wool insulation like those used in the attic of his house.

He remembered the shipwreck—the death of the *U.S.S. Exeter*—though the chronology seemed disconnected, more like a sequence of events that he'd watched on a movie theater screen. He remembered the rescue plane. "Dumbo's" were what they called the ungainly PBY Catalinas. But after that things grew increasingly fuzzy.

Something bad had happened. A terrible event.

But he did remember Margot, his wonderful wife. Her face, with those alluring French-Canadian features . . . that wave of auburn hair with the stubborn lock that always fell recklessly over one eye. God, Margot. Would he ever see her again? He had to. He must!

Lt. Vanek lay there a moment with his eyes squeezed shut, a troubled look seizing his features.

The thought came to him like an elusive firefly, flitting at the edge of his conscious thoughts.

Electroshock treatments.

He recalled reading somewhere patients weren't supposed to remember them— the smelly leather strap around his forehead, the convulsive agony shooting through his body. But he found he could remember, though the recollection kept trying to avoid him, part of the mind's way of sparing him.

He forced himself to seize the thought, embrace it. His teeth bared in a grimace, the tendons standing out on his neck.

Beyond that memory was something worse. A darkness that was trying to take form . . .

"Sir?"

The voice cut through his thoughts, snapping him into the present.

Lt. Vanek blinked quickly.

"Huh?"

He saw the orderly standing over him from the side of his bed. He was a young man, no older than eighteen or nineteen, with freckled Irish features and a wiry reddish-brown crewcut. The eyelashes were long, almost feminine. There was a clipboard in one hand and a stethoscope around his neck.

"Try to rest, sir. It's past dinner, but they usually keep something cold in the mess. I can call if you like."

"Where am I?" Lt. Vanek asked. His throat was parched. He realized he was ravenously thirsty, as if his mouth and throat were caked with salt. And hungry. In answer, his stomach let out a protesting growl.

"In a safe place," the orderly replied. "You've been through quite an ordeal. You need to rest first. The doctor can explain everything."

Lt. Vanek didn't have a lot of experience in hospital wards, but he knew enough to pick up that something wasn't right here. The restraints, for starters. And the evasive non-answers.

"I-I need to contact my commanding officer," he said, forcing the words out. His lips were dry and cracked. "Colonel Halstead. Is he here?"

"It's all been taken care of," the orderly said.

Lt. Vanek eyed him warily, all at once aware of something else, a subliminal awareness he didn't recall possessing before. Almost tangibly he gleaned the man's weakness, his fears. His name was Liam Cunningham, private first-class, and he was one of those closet homosexuals Lt. Vanek had heard about. Cunningham was terrified about the military finding out. Surprisingly, Lt. Vanek found that didn't bother him. Not after what he'd seen working in Intelligence. What did bother Lt. Vanek was what else he saw: Private Cunningham had on more than one occasion indulged himself while peeking at the anatomy of his male patients when they were out, or he thought they were out. Sometimes fondling his patients. It was the closest he'd come to indulging his sexual orientation.

A *pervert*!

But the turmoil of fear and conflict around him was the most overriding thing Lt. Vanek was aware of. It was almost palpable in the surrounding air.

"Can I get some water?" Lt. Vanek asked.

"Of course!" Pvt. Cunningham answered, a hint of a smile on his lips, which were moist and thin. There was an oily smarminess to it Lt. Vanek didn't care for at all. One that made him feel dirty just by looking at it.

Putting the clipboard down, Pvt. Cunningham reached over to the nightstand by the bed and taking the pitcher that was there, poured a little into the glass next to it.

Lt. Vanek raised his head slightly as the water was tipped into his mouth. Even as the blessed water eased over his tongue and throat, the darkness that had been hovering at the edge of his consciousness bloomed suddenly.

Pvt. Cunningham let out a gasp and took a step backward. At the moment of contact something had connected, leapfrogged from Lt Vanek's mouth across the glass and up the orderly's arm, with the speed of [an electric shock] thought.

Lt. Vanek saw the man's eyes momentarily flash silver blue, the smile stretching into a hideous grin. The free hand wandered toward Lt. Vanek's groin.

"No! Not that!" Lt Vanek hissed. "The restraints. Release them!"

Pvt. Cunningham's grin faltered, but his hand moved instead to Lt. Vanek's side.

"Of course," the orderly responded, his voice now taking a robotic quality. "A man should be free. Free to do as he pleases," he added, cryptically.

Lt. Vanek forced himself to remain still while the restraints were undone.

"I agree," he said, once they were. Then in one swift motion, he snatched the heavy porcelain pitcher and swung it, connecting with the side of Pvt. Cunningham's head with a meaty thud. The orderly's eyes rolled up and he collapsed.

From the front room, the radio started playing a newer tune by Tommy Dorsey.

Minutes later he was dressed in Cunningham's uniform. Though a little short in the sleeves and pant cuffs, it was close enough to pass muster, at least in the dark. But he'd have to move quickly to get out of here.

The 'here' was quickly established from the I.D. in Cunningham's pockets: Camp Hero Air Force Base. Along with a rail pass, a half-pack of Lucky Strikes, a Zippo lighter and twenty-four dollars and thirty-seven cents.

Cunningham was probably going to wake up with one hell of a headache. Lt. Vanek dressed him in his hospital robe and bound him in the bed, tightly. Give him a taste of his own medicine. For good measure he tore off a piece of sheeting and shoved it in his mouth as a gag.

Lt. Vanek's plan was simple: somehow get word to his commanding officer here. Then back to Margot, at the house in Larchmont. To do that, however, he'd need to get past the security checkpoints and to the train station here in Montauk, which was roughly five miles away.

Then he'd have to make his way to Larchmont, without getting caught.

From the clock in the front room it was already 5:30 a.m. It wouldn't be dawn until after seven. But the base would already be waking up. In the front room he saw on the desk there were two cups of coffee, along with a fresh manila envelope. Both cups were warm. Lt. Vanek's guess was there was a more senior ranking soldier in charge, who perhaps had stepped out to grab some early chow. Aside from a couple of desks and chairs, a magazine rack and closet-sized bathroom, the room was spartan. Outside the front door he could see there was a soldier standing guard, the pale light reflecting off the M-1 Garand slung over his shoulder.

Lt. Vanek had no idea if the trick he used on Private Cunningham would work here or not, but he had to devise some way to get past him. Quickly. The uniform and darkness might buy him an element of surprise.

The envelope drew his attention.

Inside were the kind of documents he recognized: reports on test results from a classified Research and Development project. There also several small photos of a destroyer-style chair inside a square, metal mesh cage.

Something about the chair and cage struck him as ominous. Repulsive.

Even worse: the last few pages were incident reports.

About himself.

Lt. Vanek closed his eyes a moment. According to the report, seven men had died already. By inexplicable phenomena linked to his presence. The report referenced others that weren't included.

Equally disturbing were the summaries about the chair and chamber construction, which had been going on for months.

The design had been developed by none other than Anton Kovacs. According to the dates and notes it had gone on *after* his disappearance. The irony wasn't lost on Vanek. The man he had been assisting had been orchestrating his demise.

At the bottom, the construction requisition had been approved by—of all people—Colonel Halstead.

His commander.

What the hell was going on? Were these two technologies connected? Was his doomed mission aboard the *U.S.S. Exeter* somehow anticipated?

How could this have been going on right here at Camp Hero without his knowing?

He thought a moment. He'd never been in the infirmary but had passed by countless times. Which meant Colonel Halstead's office was only a few hundred yards away to the southwest. If he was in today. But what day was it?

With that came a more troubling thought: how could he have been held here against his will after surviving the wreck of the *Exeter*, without Colonel Halstead not knowing about it?

Because he *did*, dummy.

Halstead signed the reports.

He started to glance through the reports again but was interrupted by the crunch of footsteps on gravel outside, followed by a muffled greeting. Looking around, Lt. Vanek saw there was no place to hide, though it was dimly lit with only a single overhead light and a desk lamp in the room.

Think!

The doorknob began to turn . . .

He did the only thing he could think of: he dashed into the seat by the desk, kicked his feet up and ducked his head behind the newspaper like he was engrossed in it.

"Dammit, Cunningham, I told you to keep your feet off the desk," said the man as he entered. Something clattered on the desk out of Lt. Vanek's view as he dropped his legs, keeping the paper raised.

Lt. Vanek let out a non-committal grunt in reply.

To his surprise, it seemed to work. The other man said, "Here, I brought you a roll and some of that powdered crap they pass off as eggs at the mess. How's our patient?"

"Sleepin'," muttered Lt. Vanek, in what he hoped was an approximation of Cunningham's voice.

"Good. Brass is coming through at 0800 to check on our progress, so look smart. Halstead says the chair'll be ready this morning—they're gonna put that lunatic in the frying pan and see what happens when they switch on the juice. Crazy stuff. I gotta take a leak."

A second later the bathroom door closed and Lt. Vanek heard the man whistling as he relieved himself. Struck by an inspiration, Lt. Vanek dropped the paper and lit up a cigarette. The trick was to get past the guard. He was banking on the dark and bluster working in his favor.

There was only one option left now: get back to Margot. There was extra money back at the house. Maybe they could find a way to escape north into Canada until he could figure this whole thing out.

"Be right back," he said, just loud enough. Odds were a man taking a leak and whistling wasn't going to focus on his voice. Grabbing one of the creased 'side caps' off the coat rack, he jammed it down on his head and marched out the door like he owned the place.

The sentry didn't even blink at him as he strutted past, pulling on his cigarette and blowing it out the side of his mouth to obscure his features. He paused in the shadow of building about a dozen yards away, looked up at the sky and took a second pull on the cigarette. In a glance he noted the position of the stars overhead—in particular the Big Dipper—and followed its position to the North Star. Toward his left he saw the 100-foot radio tower barely a hundred yards away. Behind him to the east was the second tower. Camp Hero was on the southern shore of Long Island and the entrance gates were on the north, along the main highway: Route 27. Or Montauk Boulevard as the locals called it.

The next question was how to get past the main sentry gate and down the road without being discovered. Which posed another problem: if the sentry behind was paying attention, he couldn't just waltz off the base.

"Hey, pal," said a voice just a couple yards to his side. "Got a light?"

Startled, Lt Vanek turned as a figure emerged out of the gloom. A stocky-looking man with a moon-shaped face stepped up to him. Lt. Vanek noted the technical sergeant stripes on the arms.

"Sure, Sergeant," he replied, pulling out the Zippo lighter. Cupping his hand around it against the wind, he flicked the flint wheel.

In the waving glow of the flame he saw the man eyeing him carefully.

"Say . . . you look awfully familiar, *Private*," the sergeant said, leaning in to light his cigarette. The voice had a southern drawl to it.

"Nope. Just got here, sir," Lt. Vanek said, aware he'd missed the proper form of address the first time. He snapped the lighter shut before the sergeant could study him further—he was sharp enough to pick up the single private strip on the uniform in the dark.

"That's funny, there haven't been any new arrivals here in weeks. I outta know, I'm the base quartermaster. I'm sure I've seen you around here. You have a name?"

Lt. Vanek tried to think quickly, but nothing came. "Private Cunningham," he said after a pause.

"Like hell—" the Sergeant shot back, cut off as Lt. Vanek's hand went to his throat. He began to struggle then stopped, his voice turning to a dying gurgle. His hands grabbed at Lt. Vanek's but without any real force: what he was seeing filled him with paralyzing horror, something the sergeant wasn't easily prone to.

The instant after Lt. Vanek came in contact with him, he saw 'Private Cunningham' transform into a bizarre version of his dead grandmother, one with a half-rotting skull fused with a catfish that he'd fished out of a local creek as a kid, a real nasty monster who'd clamped down on his fingers and nearly torn them off. And the eyes, the glowing blue-silver eyes that seemed to seize his willpower and dissolve it away like battery acid.

The cigarette tumbled out of his mouth and landed on the sandy soil in a tiny explosion of embers. The sergeant's eyes went wide and wider still, his mouth going slack.

Just as disturbing, along with the horror of what he was doing to another human being, Lt. Vanek couldn't deny an intoxicating thrill; the feeling of incredible power, the ability to crush another's will simply through one of his hands.

And yet . . . with it came a self-loathing he'd never experienced. A repulsive aftertaste of corruption like the time he'd bitten into a seemingly fresh apple that had part of the core rotted. Overriding this though, was something far more basic: survival. He had to get away from here at any cost.

Glancing about, he could just see the sentry still standing under the light of the infirmary. For the first time in his military service, Lt. Vanek was grateful to see someone who was lousy at their job.

From nearby came the sound of a Jeep approaching, its shielded headlights casting muted beams along the road. Lt. Vanek dragged the sergeant's body over behind a nearby bush and searching him, took his .45 sidearm and papers.

The Jeep came around a bend and came to a stop. Lt. Vanek tucked the gun behind into his waistband and stood at the ready.

Two soldiers were in front, though he could make out little in the dim light.

"Waiting for a lift into town, soldier?" the driver asked, much to Lt. Vanek's surprise.

"Yes, sir," he replied, snapping off a salute.

"Hop in."

Lt. Vanek didn't hesitate. He stepped around back and clambered into the back seat. To his further surprise, the guard at the sentry box didn't even ask for his papers. He simply saluted and raised the bar to let them drive through.

The driver turned left onto Montauk Boulevard—Route 27—and once on the concrete highway, gunned the throttle. Lt. Vanek sat back and enjoyed the momentary respite, one hand holding his hat in place as the salt air whipped at his face. It was the kind of night Lt. Vanek could imagine taking his wife out for a romantic drive. Instead he was sneaking away from a base that had . . .what? What had they done to him?

They'd gone a few hundred yards down past the last sentry house when Lt. Vanek caught the distant bray of the base siren going off. At first, he wasn't sure if the men in front caught it as well—the engine of the Jeep was rather noisy—then the driver cocked his head and downshifting, pulled over to the side of the road. To the east, the first hint of light was appearing on the horizon, the sky filled with wispy grey cumulus clouds chasing overhead.

"Colonel, did you hear that?" the driver said.

"Yep, Major, I sure did. Guess we'd better—"

There was a dull click of the slide on the .45 being worked, followed by the cold kiss of the barrel at the back of the colonel's neck.

Colonel Halstead? Could it be?

"Keep driving," Lt. Vanek ordered in a steady voice, "or the colonel's brains will be all over the windscreen. Clear?"

When the driver instinctively tried to glance backward, Lt. Vanek prodded the colonel's neck, hard.

"Drive," he hissed.

"Whatever you say, mister," the driver said, putting the Jeep back in gear and easing back onto the road. The colonel remained silent, staring fixedly ahead.

It went that way as they covered the next mile, Lt. Vanek keeping his eye on the driver. Even in the dim light there was something about his body language he didn't like, or perhaps it was in his thoughts, those that he found himself picking up on (but not as readily as the men back at the base, he noted).

Coming down the hill from the area of Camp Hero, the Jeep picked up speed.

"Where you want to go, mister?" the driver asked. He practically yelled over the sound of the engine and wind.

Lt. Vanek almost blurted out 'to the train station' but checked himself.

"I need a boat," he lied. They were coasting along the stretch where, past the phragmites lining the shoreline, could be seen the expanse of Montauk Harbor to the north. Lt. Vanek's knowledge of the geography here was scant, but he had visited the base a year previous, briefly.

Lt. Vanek was alerted by a sudden movement in the driver's head—a snap glance to the side as he wrenched the steering wheel toward the entrance of a dirt road. He never knew what prompted the driver to attempt any heroics, but it proved to be a fatal mistake. The man twisted around as he spun to a stop, making a play for the gun. Instead, Lt. Vanek knocked his arm aside and shot him point-blank in the face.

The colonel, perhaps thinking discretion was the better part of valor, put his hands up in the air.

"Don't shoot!" he cried.

Lt. Vanek trained the gun on him. "Get out. Slowly. Don't turn around."

The colonel eased one foot out of the Jeep, then another, Lt. Vanek following him, carefully.

"There's no place you can escape to, Lieutenant," the colonel said over his shoulder, in a measured voice. "You'll be gunned down like a dog before you get half a mile."

Lt. Vanek had a different opinion on that, but there was no point discussing it.

"What's going on? What happened to me, sir!?"

"Why don't we go back to the Camp, sit down and discuss it like reasonable men?"

Like Private Cunningham, Lt. Vanek picked up the images and thoughts behind the other man's words. Not as clearly as before, but enough.

Colonel Halstead was lying through his teeth.

About everything. Even the mission aboard the *U.S.S. Exeter*.

Something terrible had happened back there and it wasn't over yet. An experiment of sorts, a double one, actually.

"Stop," he said, once they were a few steps from the Jeep. From Camp Hero came the klaxon-bell of alarms. Even from this distance the place was lighting up like a Christmas tree.

He had to get answers.

"Tell what the—" Lt. Vanek began, then Halstead spun around with an agility Lt. Vanek wouldn't have suspected in the old man. The colonel's hands grabbed his wrists as the gun went off again. The two men pirouetted in a bizarre dance, feet kicking up sand. Lt. Vanek felt the killing urge take over again; darkness seeped through his thoughts, lending power to his hands. He wrenched his arms in a half circle, freeing them, then struck the colonel across the face, hard enough to knock several teeth out. Halstead crumpled to his knees, toppling into the coarse grass by the road.

Vanek bent down, placing one hand on Halstead's face.

Closing his eyes, mouth set in a grimace, he sent his most terrible thought into the man's mind.

Remember!

The colonel groaned, blood trickling out of his mouth and nose.

Leaving him, Lt. Vanek rolled the dead driver out and jumped behind the wheel. From the base came the sounds of multiple vehicles. He had no idea what the train schedule was for the railroad, but at least he had the Jeep.

Margot.

If it was the last thing he did on his earth, it would be seeing her one last time.

Or die trying.

He put the Jeep into gear with a clang and hit the gas hard enough to spin the back tires.

6.

NOVEMBER 1ST, 1943 0800 HOURS

It was after eight in the morning when Lt. Vanek pulled up before his house in Larchmont. It seemed like a hundred years ago since he'd been there last. The weather had turned foul—cold sleet had kicked in past Deer Park—and by the time he pulled into the drive he was soaked to the skin.

He didn't care.

Margot was all he cared about.

It wasn't until he got to the back door that it occurred to him, he didn't have the key.

Fortunately, Margot was up. She answered the door after less than a minute of pounding.

She was so surprised she nearly dropped the cup of steaming coffee in her hand.

"*John*!? I thought you were . . .?"

Lt. Vanek pushed past her, guiding her with him by the elbow. He didn't know how long he had before the authorities showed up, but he figured it wouldn't be very long. He checked the documents in the leather satchel. Some were wrinkled with damp, but the photos were good.

Margot looked at him with alarm. Even first thing in the morning, hair all mussed and face puffy with sleep, he thought she looked like a movie star. Rita Hayworth in a bathrobe, maybe.

He had to clench his teeth to keep them from chattering.

"Look at you, you poor thing! You're soaked!" she said, touching his cheek.

He realized water was pooling at his feet on the slate floor of the foyer.

"Honey, I'm afraid I don't have much time," he said, dropping the satchel and unbuttoning his shirt. He paused to give her a hard hug and kiss her on the lips.

Margot was both pleased and alarmed.

Setting the coffee aside, she helped him undress. She worked full time as a nurse at White Plains Hospital and immediately she was all business. "Time or no time, you need a hot shower. And dry clothes. How did you . . . good God, is that blood on your shirt? What are those marks on your body!?"

"I'll explain later." Standing in his jockeys he handed her the soaked bundle of clothes. "Burn these. In the furnace."

Margot looked mortified. "Burn your *uniform*?"

"It's not mine," Lt. Vanek said, hopping up the stairs with the satchel under his arm.

He took a quick, steaming shower to get his body heat back up then dug out one of his spare dress uniforms from his closet and laid it out on the bedroom chair. Then, dressed in his bathrobe, he took the satchel down to his office and laid them out on his desk. The three photos he set aside after penciling a note on one of them.

Then he took out a blank sheet of paper and laid it in front of him, staring off into space as he turned over the events of the last forty-eight hours in his mind. His hand rubbed the side of his head, absently. Then he snatched a pen from its desk holder and shaking it to draw ink to the nib, began writing.

Margot appeared in the door with a little tray of food.

"I was already making breakfast. You look like you haven't eaten in days." She rushed over and setting it down, stepped over to him. "Darling, what's happened? Tell me."

Lt. Vanek didn't answer right away. Instead, he pulled a clean manila envelope from a lower drawer and stuck the photos and most of the documents into it. He wrote out an address on it and pasted a bunch of stamps in the upper corner. Then he took the rest of the papers and shoved them back into the satchel.

He looked up at her, his expression haunted.

"It's bad business, Margot. From all sides. The secret program I was on—the one I can't really tell you about—went south. A lot of men are dead. Even worse, because of it the Navy has turned *me* into part of the experiment. I escaped. But it's only a matter of time before they track me down. I came back . . . to see you. And to mail this to the press."

Margot looked stricken, but she didn't flinch. Snatching one of his cigarettes from his desk, she lit it up and crossed her arms.

"Tell me what I can do to help."

"Give me a minute. I need to get dressed."

She blew smoke up in the air, in that arched eyebrow way only certain women can pull off, then stubbed out the cigarette and left.

He waited until she was out of the room, then stepped over to the sideboard and poured himself a stiff belt of scotch. He'd never had a drink this early in his life before, but he figured it was probably going to be his last. After a moment of contemplation, he took the manila envelope and stuffed it behind a set of oversized books in his bookcase, then left the satchel on the floor as if he'd just dropped it there in a hurry.

He picked a couple of sausages off the breakfast plate, chugged the glass of orange juice and headed upstairs.

Margot was gazing out the window of the bedroom at the intermittent traffic on Chatsworth Avenue at a neighborhood that would never look the same again. The uncertainty of war had seemed far away, even with her husband a commissioned officer in the Navy. Now that uncertainty (and the dreadful implications behind his words) had permeated the safe haven of their home.

'What about Colonel Halstead?" she asked as Lt. Vanek came into the room. Not just his commanding officer—Margot played bridge with his wife every Tuesday and the two men belonged to the same yacht club.

Vanek grunted. He walked over to her and put his arms on her shoulders.

"He *signed* the orders. To experiment on me. They rescued me from the *U.S.S. Exeter* . . . she sank off Montauk. Something happened with the experimental technology we were testing—code-named "Neptune's Reckoning". Something awful. I'm the only survivor. They're going to come for me."

He felt the tension leak out of her shoulders as the truth of that hit home. A single tear ran down her cheek. She turned and let him circle his arms around her.

"What are we going to do, John?"

He considered that a moment. He was far too exhausted to run, that much he knew. Whatever they'd done to him had left him drained, not to mention the shipwreck, and the . . . he forced the image of those last horrible moments on the destroyer out of his head. And killing military personnel? That was an automatic death sentence.

All he wanted right now was to spend a few precious minutes with the woman he loved.

He managed a weak smile.

"Lie down with me a moment, would you?"

"Of course," she said, picking up on that instant non-verbal shorthand only truly intimate couples have.

The satiny feel of her slip as his hand went to her breast triggered a response—and urgency—in both of them. Her breath quickened as his fingers touched her nipple, her own hand reaching down into his boxers. Tentative at first, then with confidence.

For the next ten minutes, Lt. Vanek lost himself in a world defined by erotic touch and sensation.

Afterward, he thought about getting up to have a cigarette, but in his current state the number of steps back down to his study seemed more a matter of miles rather than feet. Instead, he relished the low-banked warmth of Margot's lithe body snuggled up to his, the sheets and blanket a cocoon shrouding them from a world gone mad.

The face gazing up at the ceiling was impassive, but behind the brown eyes the mind was racing in all directions, like a hunted rabbit dodging this way and that.

There's a war right now in Europe, in Africa, and plenty of war over in Asia, and in all the oceans in between. Somewhere, closer to home, is something even more horrible than all that. Something far beyond anything I could have ever imagined. For God's sake, I watched it devour a United States destroyer, and all its crew.

I survived that. And God knows what else they did to me out at that base! Damn Colonel Halstead—damn him to hell!

With any luck there'd be time for a quick smoke later, he decided.

It was less than seven minutes later when he heard the pounding on their front door.

7.

NOVEMBER 9TH 1943, 1330 HOURS

"Is it ready, or isn't it?" the colonel asked, speaking slowly to enunciate his words and minimize the lisp. Since the incident with Lt. Vanek he had difficulty controlling his facial muscles. Particularly his tongue.

The nicotine from the cigarettes seemed to help, though.

Anton Kovacs—or as he was known here in the secret complex of *Bunker 18* as 'The Mad Hungarian'—stood hunched over the main console of the control room, fiddling with the dial settings. His half-mumbled, broken way of talking grated on Halstead's nerves.

"Hmm, well . . . it took some time to calibrate such a low frequency, just so! You think this is simple? There's a lot we don't understand about the fear dynamic yet! And the chair . . . it is still just a prototype. A wonderful prototype-the first of its kind! A truly revolutionary piece of equipment!

But we must be careful. We still don't understand how it ties into—"

Halstead cut him off with a wave of his hand. "A simple yes or no."

"Ready? *Ready?* Look at me! I am working day and night—"

Goddamn crazy Hungarian! he thought, tempted to pull out his .45 and put a bullet in the man's brain, if only to stop him from prattling on.

"Enough!" Halstead interrupted, glaring at the man. He didn't care for the edginess in his tone. By nature, Colonel Halstead liked to project a cool, calm demeanor, even in the midst of the most grotesque tasks of his position. But this whole situation was edging along catastrophe. Too many consecutive, sloppy mistakes.

From the initial reports he'd expected Dr. Kovacs to be meticulous, professional and buttoned up. Instead, the man he was saddled with was slovenly, prone to distraction and always running off on scientific tangents that baffled the team. In short, an overly brilliant mind unhindered by traditional scientific method: the worst kind of scientist.

Throw in a wild card like Lieutenant Vanek and you had a project that played out like a wobbly roller-coaster.

Privately, Colonel Halstead hated everything about the lieutenant: his successful lifestyle, his lovely wife, his naïve optimism and privileged self-assurance. Most of all, however, it was how Vanek consistently broke the rules and got away with it. Halstead could deal with the austere, cheerless house waiting for him back in Oklahoma when all this was done (and the cheerless but devoted, doting wife awaiting him in it—though that might be up for re-evaluation when she faced the reality of her now damaged husband) and confidence, but breaking the rules?

That was strictly forbidden in the Halstead Book of American Upbringing.

Unlike his own father, Halstead couldn't order Vanek to drop his pants, bend over and take a dozen vicious lashes with the belt.

But he could make him pay in other ways. After this latest incident, he would make Vanek pay. Dearly.

"Three p.m." he said quietly, to Kovacs. The left side of his face twitched. By the door the two guards shifted on their feet.

"That is nowhere near enough time!" Kovacs protested.

"Make it enough time, then."

Outside he lit a Lucky Strike and blew smoke up into the cool November morning.

He'd grown to hate this deserted, God-forsaken end of Long Island with its ramshackle fishing village, endless ocean and barren stretches. It felt bleak, naked and vulnerable.

At least it was well away from prying eyes.

That was important. Bunker 18 was Top Secret–only a select few on the base knew of its existence. The construction crew consisted of German POWs whose remains would never be found. If this latest development succeeded, it was possible they could wipe out Hitler's armies and bring Germany to her knees within a year.

Maybe less.

He would be a hero, saving millions of lives.

Or not. It was unlikely the United States government would want too much scrutiny on the Neptune's Reckoning project and the means used to implement it. At this point, even the President wasn't aware of it.

It was that highly secret.

But that was fine, too. It suited his sense of duty and self-sacrifice.

Regardless, once the Neptune's Reckoning project was completed, he was going to put in for a transfer. Preferably to Washington or maybe even the West Coast.

At least Lieutenant Vanek was safely under control, heavily sedated and being watched by six guards.

There'd be no screw-ups this time.

"What about the *U.S.S. Exeter*?"

Halstead glanced to his side to see Stan Krepshaw, hands clasped behind his back. Krepshaw didn't have any official military rank, but he had a high level of authority and security clearance, which had Halstead mystified. He acted in a supportive role to the project, yet his name never appeared on any documents. Krepshaw had been assigned to him early on by his superior in Naval Intelligence, with explicit orders not to ask him any personal questions.

One of those ghost string-pullers that always manages to appear in upper bureaucracy. In this case, a particularly repulsive one.

"What about it?"

"An entire destroyer lost with all hands except one, right off the coast here? With top secret technology?"

"I've taken care of it. The *Exeter* was lost with all hands a hundred miles out in the Atlantic after being torpedoed by a German U-Boat."

Krepshaw lit up a cigarette, using a gold-plated lighter. "There's still the issue of what really sank it. Any further information?"

"Ran afoul of a wolfpack is our best guess. Most likely the magnetic coating and unstable power draw led to a catastrophic event—there was concern about that early on. That was why chose one of our mothballed destroyers."

"And yet . . . no trace?"

Colonel Halstead shook his head. "Oh, there *were* traces. Over the past week a few dozen bodies have turned up on the beaches, along with debris that we recovered."

He didn't elaborate. Some of the debris had very curious damage to it, like the life preservers with suction mark holes and the body parts with giant teeth marks in them. Protocols be damned, he had ordered everything put into a pile at a remote section of the base and burned.

"But you've seen to it?"

"Of course."

Krepshaw blew smoke out his nostrils, the sunlight glinting off his frameless glasses. For a fleeting moment Colonel Halstead thought he looked like a diminutive version of the devil. Which wasn't far from the truth.

"Good. I look forward to the results of today's test. Oh, and one more thing."

"Yes?"

"This operation is now *Code: Deep Blue*. Understood?"

Colonel Halstead nodded.

"Understood."

No loose ends, then, he thought. Pity. *Margot Vanek was such an attractive woman. He wouldn't miss the mad Hungarian, though.*

Over at the "Infirmary B" building, Lieutenant Vanek lay in a stupor. Shot full of Spirobarbital, the effect was of floating in a deep, rolling sea of tepid water. In his case, one with distant, angry flashes of lightning on the surrounding horizon.

Beyond here there be dragons, he mused, a dreamy smile tugging at his lips.

A deeper part of his consciousness struggled to rally, to fight, gripped by the terror of being led helplessly like a lamb to the slaughter. But it was muted, hobbled. The dragons lurking in the mists of that horizon were far, far worse it knew, than any horror imagined by any medieval mapmaker.

Glassy-eyed, Lieutenant Vanek tilted his head, vaguely aware of the line of drool leaking down his cheek onto the pillow.

In the room with him, the six soldiers watched over him, stone-faced, armed not just with guns but ash baseball bats. All six were combat veterans from the North Africa campaign. Their orders were specific: do not shoot the prisoner if he showed signs of trouble—club him senseless. If the doctor couldn't sedate him again first.

Still, though none would outwardly admit this, since arriving in this room each felt low level, terror-riddled thoughts plucking at their minds, tailored to their individual experiences. For one, it was the Moroccan girl getting gang-raped and cut to pieces by several soldiers, for another the Vichy French officer he'd strangled with his bare hands turning black with worms erupting from his mouth.

In the room outside, the base doctor sat at his desk, smoking, two loaded syringes next to his elbow on a tray. One was a highly concentrated sedative, much stronger than Spirobarbital.

The other contained cyanide.

This time if the situation went south, he might only have a split second to make a decision.

The cyanide was the closest of the two.

He was uneasy with keeping the patient above ground here in an open ward, but the Hungarian 'doctor' was insistent he be kept away from the Bunker 18 facility as long as possible. Something about the 'proximity' to the chair he was concerned about.

The doctor—Carol Webley—was also concerned by his own proximity to the patient. In the two days since Lt. Vanek was recaptured, he'd been plagued by headaches and unpleasant thoughts.

Disturbing thoughts.

Like the recurring one where he took both syringes and plunged them into his eyes while laughing hysterically.

Clenching his teeth, he forced himself to focus again on the Stars and Stripes paper he was holding, unaware he was lighting up another cigarette only seconds after stubbing out the last one.

Off the shore of Montauk, where the continental shelf dropped away into the cold abyss of the deep Atlantic, metal groaned as the ghostly wreck of the *U.S.S. Exeter* shifted. It was wedged at the top of a crevasse known as the 'Hyborean Canyon'.

Fortunately, its oil tanks hadn't ruptured, though there was little sign of anything living in the immediate area. Bits of corpses drifted this way and that in the current along with other debris, but no predators feasted on them: two days previous, the Navy had carpeted the area with depth charges.

Most of the sea life had been either obliterated or fled.

They would return—life always did—but for now the ocean was eerily dead.

Except for a faint glow coming from the savaged front end of the destroyer.

In its doomed trajectory to the bottom, the ship had narrowly missed the much older wreck of a British man-o-war and as fate would have it, smashed into the site of a much, much older wreck of an utterly different kind of ship that no human could possibly imagine.

Locking them in what would become a symbiotic embrace.

The alien creature that inhabited it was shutting down.

At the moment, it was more-or-less sealed in by the bow of the destroyer above it, which was not a bad thing, given its wounded and severely weakened state.

The odd signals from the ship had snapped it prematurely out of its hibernation cycle and summoned it. What drew it was the peculiar frequency, though it didn't think of it in those terms.

When it arrived, tapping into the combined tensions and fear of the hundreds of life forms on board was irresistible, feeding into its matrix exponentially, enabling it to mutate at an unprecedented rate.

Its dissipation was nearly as quick as its explosive growth, retreating with alarm as the ship it attacked came down upon its nest pod. Then came the explosions, sending impact waves through the whole area, scrambling nervous systems, sending behavioral patterns into disarray, destroying life.

Damaged, the creature sealed itself again to resume its hibernation state, its alien metabolism cycling down, even as it remained aware on a different level (or channel, as it were) of the unusual connection it had made to one of the life forms, the seed it had implanted in an unprecedented way . . .

One hundred and forty miles away, Margot Vanek snapped awake in her bed, puffy-eyed and shaking, a cold sweat on her brow. Afternoon light slanted through the window curtains.

Since the morning the Naval MPs and Intelligence boys had shown up and taken her husband away, after turning the house upside down, she hadn't slept more than an hour or two at a snatch. The cavernous house on Chatsworth Avenue felt like a tomb. One that had been raided.

Violated.

Although she'd grown accustomed to her husband's long absences with the war on, this time it felt like he had been ripped out of her life forever.

By the same country he'd so loyally served, no less.

In the days following, after explicit orders from the military not to discuss the incident with anyone, especially the press, she considered suicide several times. Mainly, it was the presence of her mother and sister—who came to stay with her—and the doses of Pentothal prescribed by the family doctor that kept her from taking her life.

That, and the certain knowledge that she was pregnant.

It was far too early to know for sure, of course, but on some deeper level, she simply *knew*.

She found it both comforting . . . and unsettling.

John had been *weird* that last night they'd been together, beyond the direness of his situation: a darkness she'd never sensed before. Margot Vanek had never been 'gifted', say in the same way her grandmother was, but she'd always be sensitive to certain aspects of people that remained shielded to the rest. She could look at a stranger on the street and suddenly think: *he's hiding money from his wife because of her drinking*, or *that doctor just lied about why his patient died* . . . and later discover it was true.

Their final act of lovemaking had been strange – he'd touched her in places that made her wild with pleasure yet simultaneously *dirty* . . . like a whore. Or at least as she imagined such things.

Stress . . . I'm sure it was simply due to the stress he was under . . . unsettled his mind . . . led him to insert his . . .

Lying in bed with her husband that final time in the deceptively warm cocoon of their bed she'd shivered, a deep atavistic response to something she couldn't put her finger on.

Something about her husband terrified her.

And part of that terror might now be carried inside.

8.

NOVEMBER 9TH, 1943, 1435 HOURS

Lieutenant Vanek was in a dream.

He was on the makeshift sailboat he'd constructed as a teenager, navigating down the Allegheny River near his childhood home in Oil City, Pennsylvania. It was a brilliant summer day, the kind where sunlight sent glittering sparks off the waves that gave the muddy water a magic, ethereal quality.

The tree-covered banks to either side were the deep, rich green of mid-July, dozing in the afternoon sunlight. Further down past the Pennsy Bridge he could just make out the oil wells poking up like a battery of siege towers.

It was the kind of day he always associated with weekends of his youth: the hours an endless vista to be savored like a sweet dessert, the kind his Hungarian grandmother would make on Sundays. Despite the threadbare existence of the Great Depression, he'd never been happier in his life. Even years later, after pulling his family out of poverty into an upscale life and home in Larchmont.

On the right bank he could see several kids fishing off a dock near the railroad tracks—two boys and two girls. One of the girls was jumping up and down waving at him, pointing her pole in the direction of the bridge.

Vanek smiled, soaking in the dreamy contours of his memory. The crude canvas tarp he'd rigged as a sail tugged at the mast as the wind picked up, the little boat canting to port. As it did, he saw a disturbance in the water, twenty or thirty yards ahead.

Quite a large one in fact—a sort of whirlpool. With flailing objects appearing and disappearing.

It was growing.

Glancing over he realized that the girl who looked suspiciously like his cousin Rita, wasn't excited: she was trying to warn him.

Screaming.

Standing up in the stern, he saw that he was sailing straight toward it.

Alarmed, he yanked the rudder toward him, paying out the main sheet to let the sail fill.

Impossibly, neither had any effect.

He still continued to sail directly at the growing whirlpool, which was deepening like a drain. The water within it was turning a sickly, purplish black color as if the whirlpool was tainting the river with poison.

Vanek realized he was trying to scream too but couldn't. It was as if his jaw was wired shut. It became impossible deep now: a vortex into unimaginable horrors . . . whipping wormlike appendages, mucus-lined jaws and mutilated faces. With it came a wave of unbridled terror, not of death but of a frozen, unending darkness that would obliterate any shred of warmth or peace.

The boat was disintegrating, dissolving as he was sucked downward into the abyss . . .

. . . and into the light.

Not a healing, or a resurrection, but an awakening into a new form of nightmare. One where he was equally helpless and aware, even if in a disconnected, feverish way. The overhead fluorescent lights had a stark, haloed quality as if he'd been immersed in a chlorinated pool. He was being manhandled by four guards from a stretcher into some sort of chair inside a large cage made of copper meshing.

He tried to work his mouth in protest, but they'd strapped his jaw shut. His limbs were useless as well. Not just from being strapped—his body was so relaxed and weak they must have given him a horse tranquilizer.

The dark thoughts he was reading off the guards were distant and muddled, like murky, polluted waters.

What was this place?

It was a mad scientist's laboratory, he noted, as a headpiece was secured over his skull and his forearms were strapped to the arms of the chair. Outside the cage he could see the oblong armored glass window of a control room and inside . . .

Colonel Halstead? Anton Kovacs?

What was this? Why?

His thoughts were vague, muddled. Swathed in thick gray wool. The alarm bells sounded but they were muted.

Vanek was distracted as a second chair—a heavy-duty metal one—was brought in and placed right before him. Not long after (Vanek's sense of time had taken on an elastic quality) a young man dressed in prison fatigues was hauled in and strapped into the chair. He looked German, based on the block-like features and ice-blue eyes, which was confirmed a moment later when he spoke to the guards.

"*Ich fürchte mich nicht!*" he said emphatically. Vanek sensed the prisoner wanted it to be true. Except that he repeated it several times and how behind the granite façade, Vanek could sense the seething mass of emotions like a can of agitated worms, compressed and tight.

A few of those 'emotional fear worms', as Vanek thought of them in his fugue state, seemed to elongate and reach out to his face . . . he thought he could *taste* them.

The taste was *delicious*.

Two men stepped up to the entrance of the cage. One Vanek recognized—his old friend Colonel Halstead—but the other he did not. Halstead exuded bland, military-grade thoughtlessness: a man driven by routine and adherence to ruthless logic.

The other man was the embodiment of evil.

Short, dressed in civilian clothes, his eyes were black and soulless as a coal pit. Combined with a pallid complexion and red lips, the result was like a psychotic, effeminate vampire. The face of a man who could rip steaming entrails out of a live man's gut with a little smile. The man's gaze was electric in a terrifying way: the reptilian gaze of a cobra . . . if a reptile could go insane.

Halstead was looking at Vanek with an impenetrable stare. Except . . . a slight tick in one eyelid. A thought flitted at the fuzzy perimeters of Vanek's mind. A seed. Something he'd planted in the Colonel's mind a lifetime ago.

Behind them he could see Kovacs' head bobbing up and down before shouldering past and into the confines of the cage to fuss over wires connected to Vanek's head and wrists.

Vanek wanted to scream, even send a bolt of nightmarish (disabling) thoughts into the scientist's mind but the drugs they had given him diffused any organized efforts.

He glimpsed a hypodermic needle in Kovacs' hand . . .

"Will it work?" Stan Krepshaw asked. His lips quivered as he spoke.

"Yes, yes, of course it will work!" Kovacs said dismissively. "But you want to want to get back to the control room before it does. Once I give him this, we have six, seven minutes tops before his faculties are fully capable. Believe me, you do not want to be close to him when that happens."

Krepshaw raised his chin a fraction, getting Colonel Halstead's attention as he flicked his eyes to the staff waiting outside. In addition to the guards there were two nurses and a medical doctor on standby.

"Everyone, take your positions," the colonel said, his lisp more pronounced. The one nurse was staring at Lt. Vanek and the chair he was strapped into, uncertain.

"Outside the cage is perfectly safe?" he asked Kovacs, purely for show.

"Of course! Of course! Completely shielded!" Kovacs replied.

The medical staff retreated to their seats in front of the control room. Two guards remained outside the cage, positioned ten feet away. Two more went to the door of the control room while the remainder went to the massive steel doors which had been closed and locked minutes earlier. If for any reason things went wrong, they had orders to shoot anyone who attempted to open them without the colonel's permission.

Colonel Halstead checked his watch. They were coming up on 3 p.m.

He nodded.

Kovacs tapped the veins on Vanek's right forearm, took a second to make sure the air was squeezed out of the syringe, then plunged the needle in.

All three filed out so the one guard could secure the cage door. Inside, Lt. Vanek stared at them, glassy-eyed. The German prisoner shouted something in protest but went silent. Sweat beaded on his forehead.

To the side of the control room window, a red light pulsed, bathing the front of the cage in a blood-red glow.

Like the beat of a heart.

The control room had a heavy steel door, similar to the ones used in submarines to seal airtight compartments. The room had its own independent air ventilation system from the rest of the facility.

Inside were Kovacs, one technician, Colonel Halstead and Krepshaw. The rest of the Bunker 18 personnel were outside the steel doors. The lights were dimmed to improve visibility in the main chamber.

"I am quite interested to see how your test subject responds, this time around," Krepshaw said, cupping his hands across his midsection like a priest contemplating a benediction.

"Yes. Hauptmann Otto Groenig. Also known as the 'Chopper of Kasserine Pass'. He's one of the last surviving prisoners who helped build this bunker."

"How ironic." Krepshaw raised his chin slightly. "I must say, this latest development is quite intriguing. The implications are so much more far reaching than fancy paint on ships' hulls. I see many . . . possibilities."

Colonel Halstead shifted away a few steps, not even aware he was doing it. He found Krepshaw's demeanor off.

Funny. And not in an Abbot and Costello kind of way.

"Well, we don't know what will *really* happen when we throw the switch."

"Oh yes. And that . . . *that's* what makes this so interesting," Krepshaw replied. He was practically purring. "A three-dimensional fear generator. Oh yes, I like this *very* much. I'm sure the Hauptmann will have a lot to say after he sees this. Do you think the personnel might be affected this time?"

"They might," Colonel Halstead replied. On the previous test runs not much had happened, except for several cases of vomiting and one nurse who had resigned, citing health issues.

"Good. I look forward to that too."

Kovacs elbowed his way in to make last minute adjustments on the unit in front of them.

"I hope you appreciate this more than *fancy paint*!" he snorted. "Now please take your positions. We are about to begin!"

Outside, all the personnel in the chamber took the sound-canceling ear protectors around their necks and slipped into place.

"Ready on one!" Kovacs said to his assistant on the other end of the console. Colonel Halstead and Krepshaw stood in an area taped off on the floor near the exit. The wall behind the console was lit up with meters and gauges. From the center console a series of (airtight sealed) copper conduit tubes ran up and out along the ceiling to where they dropped down into the Faraday cage. Sodium-arc lamps were positioned outside the cage illuminating it from all four sides, while three Fairchild cameras (and two 16mm film cameras) rigged with automated timers and shutter releases were positioned on tripods to capture the event.

"Roger," the assistant replied.

"*Proceed*," Kovacs said.

The assistant flipped the power switch activating the Faraday cage, which began to hum and crackle.

"Generators cycled up to full power?" asked Kovacs.

"Generators at full power," the assistant replied, leaning over to check the readings.

"Electromagnetic charge on the cage?"

"Steady. Variations within acceptable range."

"Sound?"

"Twenty hertz and steady." The assistant leaned over to check the meter and dial position. From the giant speakers high up on the wall—their cones aimed precisely at the center of the cage—came a low thrum that vibrated through the glass.

Inside the cage, Lt. Vanek suddenly tensed, his back arching as if an electrical current were being passed through it. His lips pulled pack in a rictus of pain. Across from him the eyes of the German officer who had mowed down fifty-seven American prisoners with an M-42 heavy machine gun without flinching went wide.

The film cameras began their methodical clicking, muted by the pulsing heavy drone coming through the speakers.

"Volume?" Kovacs asked. In the up lights of the panels, his craggy features took on a diabolical aspect.

"Twenty-five percent."

Kovacs checked his watch and made a note on the clipboard resting on the control board in a slot near his elbow.

"Increase to fifty."

"Roger."

The assistant slowly turned the bakelight dial to the halfway mark. Even with the armored glass and soundproofing, the metal and loose objects began to rattle inside the control room. Outside the cage shuddered. A spark flew off from the top.

Inside the cage, Lt. Vanek began to thrash. His head, locked firmly in place by the helmet, kept him looking straightforward.

Kovacs looked over at Colonel Halstead.

They'd pushed things to this level before and backed down. He'd warned him the consequences might be irreversible if they went all the way.

Halstead gave a firm nod.

"Sound to one hundred percent," Kovacs said to his assistant, his voice now shouting. "Start dropping the frequency on my command."

The assistant, a veteran of military hospitals that handled interrogation prisoners, didn't blink. His right hand went back to the frequency dial, which in addition to set frequency lines had several new ones improvised in white tape.

"Roger."

With the volume now at one hundred percent, he began to ease the frequency dial down.

Inside the cage, things began to happen.

The crystal at the center of the helmet began to glow . . . cobalt blue.

From Lt. Vanek's face, things began to *emerge*.

Otto Groenig, who had never shown fear (outwardly, at least) screamed at the top of his lungs, high and shrill. His screams were swallowed up in the deep, sonic pulse coming out of the speakers.

The lights dimmed and one of the cameras toppled over, snarling wires with it.

"What is happening?" Krepshaw asked, barely keeping the excitement out of his voice. "I can't see that well."

Colonel Halstead, whose vision was as good as any fighter pilots, could see quite clearly, even through the copper mesh. What he was seeing was mesmerizing in an utterly horrific way. Wormlike filaments were streaming out of Vanek's mouth and eyes, mutating as they did so into fantastic shapes: leering hobgoblins, satyr-faced monsters that suggested Jewish caricatures, ghoulish corpses clawing along the inside of the cage.

Of course! Part of him realized, he was witnessing physical manifestations of the German officer's fears! They'd had glimpses before, but nothing like this. *This was truly fascinating!*

Next to him, Krepshaw gasped as a flair in the lighting brought it all out in lurid detail.

Seated on the bench near the control room, the medical staff looked on in equal horror. The guards, all armed with Thompson submachine guns, gripped their weapons a little tighter.

"Colonel?" Kovacs asked from the right, a slight tremor in his voice. Both him and the assistant on the other end of the console didn't seem to be operating it as much as holding on for dear life. The power of what was unfolding was undeniable. As if to emphasize this, the walls trembled and shook.

"Yes," Colonel Halstead said through clenched teeth. "Proceed."

The assistant edged the frequency modulator dial to the final, marked position.

From inside the cage, the filaments broke free in a hideous pantomime of birth. Whatever creatures had spawned within were free. With increasing speed, they ricocheted around the inside of the cage, repelled by the electromagnetic shielding.

Except those that latched onto the German officer. His screams diminished to grunts as they tore him to pieces. Blood and gore exploded within the cage.

The butchery was brutal.

"Colonel?" Kovacs asked, his voice edged with nervousness. Several parts of the cage mesh were bent outward. Two of the arc lamps exploded, taking out the nearest film cameras.

"Seen enough?" Colonel Halstead asked Krepshaw.

"Oh, more than enough! This is positively—"

He was cut off as a tremendous *thud* came from within the chamber and the locks on the cage door flew off. The mesh door whipped across the room and decapitated one of the nurses, eviscerating (and subtracting the arm) of the second nurse next to her, who had jumped to her feet.

What was inside burst out.

And they were *hungry*.

By the massive steel doors, the guard on the left panicked. He reached for the handle on the massive deadbolt and when the other guard tried to intervene, shot him point blank. In any other circumstance, the bar of steel would have been impossible for one man to move—typically three were assigned to it—but adrenaline was so high he slid it open without thinking.

Throwing his shoulder into the steel door with every ounce of strength, he wasn't aware of the tendons being torn in his scapula as he forced it open a foot. The issue became moot a moment later when several clawed hands tore into him from behind, slashing skin and bone. He died seconds later, screaming, as several of the things poured through the gap and into the hallway beyond.

Down the corridor at the radio relay station, the operator looked up, trying to process what he was seeing rushing toward him. The screams were enough to tell him today's test had gone horribly wrong and he had been transmitting an emergency signal—"Code Red, all Bunker 18 personnel, we have Code Red!"—when he spotted several hideous flying monkeys (fanged versions of the Wizard of Oz ones he had nightmares about) closing in. Even as his bladder released in his pants, he had enough presence of mind to hit the failsafe locking mechanism on the outer doors, even as the first monkey crash landed onto his desk, scattering papers and equipment.

A moment later it bit his face off.

Inside the control room, lights flashed and several panels shorted out.

Alarmed, Kovacs reached over to hit the emergency override breaker, only to find his wrist seized by Colonel Halstead. He tried to push it anyway, to no avail.

"What are you doing!? I must stop it!"

Looking up, he saw a face that was no longer sane: in the up lights of the panel, the colonel was staring out into the control room, the whites around his eyes entirely visible, lips pulled back in a hideous grin.

Over by the door, Krepshaw stood with his palms out, blabbering "Oh . . . oh . . .oh!" Like a man in the throes of ecstasy. From outside, the intensifying drone of low frequency sound was punctuated by the staccato pop of gunfire, mixed with screams as the chamber became a slaughterhouse.

The assistant bolted up and ran to assist Kovacs and found himself grabbed by the collar as he tried to get around Colonel Halstead. Kovacs was hauled to his feet. The colonel was shaking, like a man possessed.

Inside the chamber, lights flickered on and off, several popping and exploding. The screams were muffled.

From the chair, Lt. Vanek's skull gaped, the glow from the crystal in the helmet intensifying to a blinding blue light, his eyeballs leaking blackness as his feet thrummed on the floor.

The sound reached a crescendo. The speakers shredded and blew out.

A bright light burst forward from the cage like a laser, piercing the armored glass like a molten cannonball. Inside, the lights flickered on and off as blood and body parts flew.

There was a muffled *bang* as the outer iron doors were impacted with the force of a tank.

Bunker 18 went quiet.

9.

DECEMBER 4TH, 1943 0900 HOURS

Three officers stood on a grass-covered hill over the coastal battery called 'Dunn', not far from where Colonel Halstead and Stanley Krepshaw had their conversation a month earlier.

One, a taller man with a Clark Gable mustache, was the base commander, Lieutenant General Goodrich. The other two from the Office of Naval Intelligence had been sent from Washington to handle 'damage control'. Goodrich was bristling as Camp Hero was technically an Army base and it was the Navy who was responsible for this fiasco.

Now they were trying to sweep the whole damn thing under the rug and these two suits were here giving him the old hard line lecture on how to do it. The whole thing stank. It was dirty, ugly business and the general had little stomach for it.

What the hell had Colonel Halstead been thinking? How many personnel were entombed down there?

"All access points have been sealed?" the one named McKinney asked.

"They have. All traces of Bunker 18 have been obliterated. The outer bunker has been repurposed as a secondary storage facility. Unless whatever happened down there can bust through two feet of solid concrete."

It was a typically brisk day for December, a wind from the outer banks pulling cat's paws off the wave crests. A wind that might have come all the way from war-torn Europe. Maybe even from the bitter lines of the Russian Front. Goodrich stood with hands clasped behind his back, the leather satchel tucked under his arm.

"It looked more than sufficient, sir," McKinney replied. "Those are the last of the documents?"

"Yes, all that could be found." He took the satchel and handed it over. What it contained was much heavier than the weight of it.

"Very good. Once again, sir, you are bound by the official secrets act from ever mentioning any of this to anyone. Ever."

General Goodrich's left eye squinted. He managed to keep his temper. The two men had been brisk and condescending during the cleanup.

"If that's all?" he said, indicating the path to where their car was parked. They'd insisted on a final inspection of the site before leaving. These two loved crossing their 't's and dotting their 'i's.

"Yes, sir. We'll consider the matter closed. Good day."

Watching them walk away, the wind to their backs, General Goodrich frowned. It was ugly business alright, now sealed up like a cauterized wound and forgotten. How many people died down their due to Kovacs' crackpot technology? Two dozen? More? It was too dangerous to go in and do a body count, though it seemed whatever forces had been unleashed had exhausted itself and dissipated.

They hoped.

There had only been one survivor, but he had died shortly after. The Naval Intelligence Office had sent their own ambulance to pick him up. Following the accident, the whole accident had been written off as a terrible transformer explosion, or at least that was the story circulated around the base.

General Goodrich turned away. He'd already been reassigned, as had any key personnel that might have witnessed anything or been involved.

That was fine for him. He was looking forward to a quieter desk job in Manhattan, where they were working on a new project.

Over by the supply depot, an Army Corps of Engineer Sergeant lit up a cigarette as the last of his crew piled into the 2 ½ ton truck. His name was Alfonse Scarpia. Before the war, he worked in construction in the five boroughs. He swung up into the cab next to the corporal, a kid from Detroit he'd managed to rope into his many 'supply redistribution' schemes. Mostly rationed construction equipment.

The corporal looked at his watch. They had a drop-off in Jamaica in three hours, enough time to grab a beer.

"Do you think those knuckleheads will ever figure out we only used half the concrete?" he asked the sergeant.

"Fuck no," Scarpia replied. "You think anyone is going to drill a hole and measure it? Fat chance. Nah, we're good on this. Hit the gas."

The End

Robert Stava is an author living in the Hudson River Valley, not far, apparently, from the village of Wyvern Falls where so many of his horror stories are set. His fourth and fifth novels, "Nightmare from World's End", and "Lost World of Kharamu" are published by Severed Press. His short stories have appeared in various anthologies & magazines including the recently released "Cranial Leakage vol II" from Grinning Skull Press. "Neptune's Reckoning," from Severed Press, is his ninth novel.

Originally from Cleveland, Ohio, he grew up in the Finger Lakes region of New York State and after pursuing a degree in Fine Arts, wound up making his career in advertising at Y&R and J. Walter Thompson in NYC. He went on to become Creative Director of the 3D Media Group at Arup, an international U.K-based design company before moving to the Hudson Valley and catapulting into the wild world of writing horror fiction in 2010.

In addition to writing, Stava is a trustee on the Ossining Historical Society and is professional member of ITW (International Thriller Writers) and the HWA (Horror Writer's Association).